D1282108

I, Rebekah, Take You, the Lawrences

by Julia First

A GROLIER COMPANY

Franklin Watts

New York/London/Toronto/Sydney/1981

HOUSTON PUBLIC LIBRARY

R0143806657
CCR

Library of Congress Cataloging in Publication Data

First, Julia.
    I, Rebekah, take you, the Lawrences.

    SUMMARY: Even after she has been
adopted, 12-year-old Rebekah wonders if she
wouldn't be better off back at the orphanage with
her friends.
    [1. Adoption—Fiction] I. Title.
PZ7.E49875Iar   [Fic]   80–24588
ISBN 0–531–04256–1

Copyright © 1981 by Julia First
All rights reserved
Printed in the United States of America
5   4   3   2   1

To Kiar and Mike
With love in your hearts you keep
finding room for one more

CHAPTER 1

I used to think that being poor, abandoned by your parents, and living in an orphanage was the worst thing that could happen to a person. Well, I'm not saying it's a piece of cake, but I know now that there are worse things. I won't enumerate them because that's pretty depressing, but at the top of the list is something very basic. What I'm talking about is not knowing your own strengths and weaknesses. And if you're stupid enough not to know that, then obviously you're not smart enough to recognize it in other people—and that can spell disaster. But let me start a ways back.

You see, I was raised in the Meacham County Home for Little Wanderers, and that isn't a place where the milk of human kindness gets nurtured in a person. It's self-help or you're dead. The professionals call it a "Children's Shelter," and we were referred to as "children without families" or "children who wait." That last one hurt the most because we all knew what we were waiting for but for some it never came.

Mildred Watson, my best friend in our dorm,

had all the appearance of being one of those. Mildred was handicapped. Nothing physical or mental —it was just that she always got picked on and never fought back. I guess we were all losers in a sense, but she was bad news for herself nine times out of nine. So when it wasn't against the Authority, I'd stand up for her.

"Anybody give you a hard time while I was gone, Mildred?" I checked up on her every time I got back from living with a foster family.

"No, it was okay, Rebekah." Mildred wouldn't tell me what really happened because she didn't want me to feel bad about it.

"Those villains at school?"

"Aw," and she'd shrug her shoulders.

After every one of my live-in placements, I'd swear to myself I wasn't going on another one unless Mildred could come with me so I could protect her. Needless to say, I didn't have any control over that.

"Rebekah Blount, you're being placed with the Careys."

Okay—the Careys. You pack your things, get carted away, meet new "parents," sometimes new "sisters" and "brothers," a new school, new rules.

Then—Boom! It's over.

"Rebekah Blount, you're being placed with the Smiths."

Okay—the Smiths. You pack your things, get carted away again, go through the exact same routine, and boom! That one's over too. I'd been doing this for five years.

The terrible part was that some of those places were nice. Sounds crazy, I know. The thing is, if they weren't so nice, you'd be glad when you had to leave. But when you get to like the people, become attached to them and *then* get moved, well, it's hard.

The deal is, foster parents agree to keep kids only for a specified length of time, and when the time is up that's it. I don't have anything against them for that. They do their best and they have their reasons for taking kids on a short-term basis. And you know it in advance, so it's not like they're pulling a fast one. But, like I said, when you get used to them it hurts, and with one family I didn't think I'd ever get over it.

Those were the Brownings. They had a farm, and after life in the polluted city, that farm was like the gateway to heaven.

I mean, take the smell of sheets. Now this might not mean much to someone who's never slept on sheets that come from an institutional laundry. Springtime fresh they're not. But Mrs. Browning used to hang hers out in the yard, and the sun and the country air would get so ingrained in all the threads that even after I slept on those sheets for a whole week they'd still have the same fresh smell.

And the way the Brownings acted toward me personally too was something you don't get every day. They didn't ask a million questions about what I did when I wasn't with them. They weren't like some people who push to get inside your private thoughts.

The reason they had to give me up was because of their age. They were in their fifties, and they wanted to sell their big place and get rid of all the hard work that went with it. Taking in kids got complicated, so we had to break up. After living with them, I wanted to build a wall between me and the world. I didn't want to let that heartbreak happen to me again.

At that time the enrollment at Meacham was around forty-five and honest, so far as we kids were concerned, it was like a maximum security prison. They have a bell that gets you up in the morning that could wake the dead. I mean, it sounds like armed guards are being alerted that a prisoner is trying to escape. As soon as we'd hear it we'd squash our pillows over our heads and wait until we thought the last clang was over. Then we'd count to ten—slowly—just in case.

"Mildred, it's okay. You can come out from under now."

She was always the last one to emerge. That'll give you an idea of her personality.

There are three buildings in Meacham, one for girls, one for boys, and a nursery for both sexes. The boys' and girls' buildings have two floors; the top floors are the dormitories and the first floors have a kitchen, a dining room, an activity room, and a counselor's office. The counselors are social workers who arrange foster home and adoption placements, and part of their job also is talking to you if you have some special problem that talking about is supposed to cure. I never heard of any talks at Meacham that did that, though.

The house parents were pretty good on the whole, except, unfortunately, mine. Warden is actually a better description than housemother for Baker, the one I had. Of course, never remembering what a mother was like firsthand, I couldn't swear to it, but I figure a real mother is supposed to be someone who loves you. No matter how hard you tried, you couldn't have squeezed a drop of love juice out of Baker because she didn't have even an ounce of it in her veins.

"Rebekah Blount, I see wrinkles in your bed!"

She'd uncurl the word "wrinkles," out of her mouth as if she were saying "WORMS!"

The corners of Baker's lips were trained in a permanent downward direction, making it look as if her mouth were enclosed in parentheses. I never dared give her a dirty look because of the rumor that she'd strike a kid across the face if her psyche got upset. Just looking at her, even if you never had a confrontation, would make you drop your gaze. She was huge. Not fat but big, like some men are big. She had one of those heavy treads that always let you know when she was coming down the hall. It sounded like Bigfoot. Which of course had one advantage. If you weren't doing the job you were supposed to be doing, you could hurry and look real busy.

I can still visualize Baker's ugliness. It was mostly her eyes, which were like coffee beans. You know—inanimate. About twenty kids sat at the dining room table, and we rotated places weekly so everyone had the terrific opportunity of sitting next to Baker at least twice during the month. Actually, it didn't make any difference how far away from her you sat, you were always aware of her and her coffee-bean eyes.

But it wasn't just fear that made us all hate Baker. It was her talent for making us see ourselves as rejects. She was right about that, though. We weren't all orphans. There were all kinds. Like kids whose parents hadn't gotten married or parents who were divorced and neither one wanted the kid. Some parents were in hospitals. Mental hospitals, that is. There were three like that in my own dorm and only seven girls altogether. That's a big percentage.

About my background, I couldn't tell you. I don't remember much about it. When I strain my memory I can see someone coming into my room in the middle of the night when I was around three or four years old and telling me to get dressed and hurry. After that I was in a bunch of different places with ladies I knew I didn't belong to but was told to call "Mother" anyway. I did what I was told, but I knew it wasn't real.

Then, from six on, Meacham got to be home. Not in the real sense of the word, I mean, like when you live with your family. I don't have any blood relations that I know of, but I must have had parents sometime. I mean you have to. That's how you get into this world.

With an assortment like us it was easy for someone like Baker to hurt our feelings.

"Mildred Watson, the next time your mother comes I'm going to report to her that your behavior is in great need of improvement."

She knew that Mildred couldn't have done anything wrong—Mildred was too meek. She also knew that Mildred's mother hadn't laid eyes on her for two months. That was another one of Mildred's problems. For those of us who didn't have mothers, it was bad enough. But if you did have one and she wasn't in any hospital . . . We never could understand why Mildred's mother couldn't have Mildred live with her. I still don't understand it, but at least I've learned that there are some very hard things you have to accept—like it or not.

Then Baker would keep tormenting Mildred. She'd say, "Oh, of course," like she'd just remembered. "Your mother hasn't been here for—how long is it now? Well, you'll have plenty of time to work on your conduct before her next visit."

Then she'd give her this pitying look, until Mildred would hang her head like she'd been caught stealing.

That was the kind of Authority I couldn't help Mildred with.

When Baker was cruel like that, I had so much

hate inside me that I wanted to find an iron pole. Not so heavy that I couldn't lift it, and not so long that I couldn't get a good swing with it, but just the right size and weight to be effective. I'd pick it up and wrap both my hands around it like people up at bat in baseball games, and I'd walk over to Baker and calmly pummel her and pummel her until she dropped and didn't move any more. That may be what is known as cold-blooded murder, but I've gotten great joy just thinking about it. I'd even say it gave me supreme satisfaction. I don't like to admit that I wouldn't do it for real—that takes some of the satisfaction away.

I suppose if we were to count our blessings, going to school "off campus" as they called it, was one of them. I don't mean that the school I went to was so great, but the one on campus was for kids who had problems. Not the ones we all had, which was just being a "resident" of Meacham, but the kinds of problems you need a psychiatrist for. About a third of the kids must have been like that. The school on the grounds had regular subjects but time out for sessions with the doctors. One of the girls in my dorm, Kathy Greco, was in that group. She was also one of the three kids who had a parent in a mental hospital. Her mother. Personally, I didn't think there was a thing wrong with Kathy. She was just scared she was going to get like her mother. I mean it was like an obsession, and it interfered with practically everything she did.

"Let's go shoot some baskets."

That was something we knew Kathy was good at. She was taller than any of us and scored practically all the points for our team the few times she played. That happened after she'd had a good day with her doctor. But if we made the suggestion on any other day, she'd refuse to leave our room. "No, I'll fumble the ball." She'd actually quiver and hide her face.

Or we'd say, "C'mon, Kathy, we're going down to the kitchen. We've got permission to help Christy with Mary Ellen's birthday cake."

"I can't. I—I'll mess something up." She'd shake her head so much we'd be afraid it was going to detach from her body.

Those birthdays, by some stretch of the imagination, could be thought of as another one of our blessings. Christy was a rotten cook, but his cakes were good. He'd bring them in all lit up at the end of supper, we'd sing "Happy Birthday," and everyone would go in the activity room. If nobody from the outside sent or brought in a present, you could depend on one anyway, from the Board of Directors of the Home. They had a fund for that purpose. The gift wasn't usually what you'd been dreaming about getting, that was for sure. Sometimes it was only a pair of knee socks or a scarf—you know, something practical. One time I got a pair of mittens that looked like they'd been made from recycled string. Anyway, whatever the item, it would be unwrapped and if it was a game we'd play it, or if it was clothing, it would get tried on and everyone would say how gorgeous it looked. Actually, for a while, we were able to forget where we were and why we were there. Then the party would break up, and we'd go upstairs and the truth would set in again.

I used to have what I suppose you'd call fantasies. In one my real parents worked for the C.I.A. and were on a secret mission to a country that was too dangerous for children. In fact, it was part of their cover that I had to be incognito until their job was done or it would blow the whole project. They even had to make up some fake name for me because if I kept theirs, the enemy—whoever that was— could trace them. I mean, I figured Rebekah Blount had to be a fake name. I didn't hold on to that nutty idea for too long, though. If you keep having fantasies like that and nothing happens, you can crack up.

In actual everyday life, we went to District 12 School. I never knew a school could have a personal name until afterwards. All the neighborhood kids who went there had some kind of bond with each other. The kids from Meacham weren't included. If you didn't live in a regular house, you were an outsider. If they were nice, they called us, "those kids from the Home," or, if they weren't so nice, they'd smirk and say, "the Little Wanderers." They'd get at you in lots of other ways, too.

"Miss Williams, Mildred Watson fouled me.

She pushed me and that's against the RULES!" That would be in gym during a basketball game when all of a sudden rules got to be important. All the rest of the time breaking rules was what they lived by. Mildred couldn't foul anybody. She'd be too scared, if nothing else.

But I took care of those kids who tried to get Mildred in trouble. Like, accidentally I'd trip them up and run before they could recover. Afterward I'd give them a big Cheshire-cat grin, and they wouldn't have a shred of proof against me. Mildred would find out about it, and she'd all but cry with gratitude.

One of their other favorite things would be to circulate, "Mildred Watson has head lice." She never did of course. Then they'd finish off with, "We're not hanging out with anyone from the HOME."

So we kids from the Home used to dream a lot.

"Someday we'll get let out of here."

"Yeah. Somebody will adopt us."

There'd be silence after that, because at our age we were in the hard-to-place category so we knew it wasn't very likely.

But then at night, after I'd get into bed, and when there were no more whispers in the room, I could think in the quiet. Praying, I guess it was. *Please God, let me know you're there. Get me out of here soon and for good, so I won't shrivel up and die before I even get a chance to live.*

CHAPTER 2

The day my life started to change was a Saturday. The date was July 16. It was a very small beginning, but after the whole thing was over, I made a resolution. When I grow up, whenever July 16 comes on a Saturday, I'm going to go to the Meacham County Home for Little Wanderers and make that day like Christmas for every kid there. I'll make home-cooked meals and give every single girl a brand new silk dress. Maybe that will make up for some of those crummy presents we got on our birthdays.

But that first Saturday was a long time in coming. And when it came, I wasn't even ready for it. You see, it wasn't as if I knew it was ever going to happen at all. Not like I had a contract that was supposed to come due on a certain date, and all I had to do was sit tight and be patient.

I had watched grown-up couples come to Meacham looking around and making their choices, like when you go to a cafeteria and after you examine the food on all the shelves, you select what you want. Of course, most people interested in adoptions were looking in the Nursery, Building C, because naturally, babies are more sought after than older kids. The new parents don't have to undo any bad habits the older kids might have learned in an orphanage, and babies are supposed to be cuter anyway. That's probably right, but it never made us feel any better.

Some of the kids were sure that someday their own parents would come and get them. Not me. I figured if mine got rid of me once, they meant it for good. Particularly since nobody named Blount had ever made a request to see me. Mildred used to hold out for going back with her mother, but I didn't think she had a chance, not with those appearances her mother put in once every two months. And during those visits I never could see that she contributed one thing to Mildred's peace of mind.

Not that I saw her mother the whole time, so I couldn't say what went on in the middle part of her visit. But when she came in and when she left, all she did was sob. Sob and whimper. I mean, what good did that do Mildred?

One time was a Sunday afternoon, and Madelaine Blake and I were sitting on the floor doing card tricks. Madelaine is a genuine card addict. Mrs. Watson was already a basket case even before she got into the room. Tears were running down her face, and she wrapped an arm around Mildred's shoulders and wouldn't let go. It was like *Elmer's* glue had just been spread between them and she had to keep pressing hard so they wouldn't come apart from each other. Madelaine didn't pay any attention to them. She went right on playing cards. Maybe she did it on purpose because her own mother was in a mental hospital and couldn't come at all. But I didn't have any such emotional ties, so I could handle it.

"Baby, I'll write you," her mother sniffled as she stroked Mildred's hair. "Now you keep working hard and—" With that, Mrs. Watson choked up and couldn't finish her sentence.

By some miracle, Mildred didn't cry. "Wh— When. . . ." was as far as she could get, and her lips began taking a downhill turn.

"Rebekah, pick a card, any card," Madelaine was urging me.

I snapped my attention back to what we'd been doing. "Uh, let's go down to the activity room," I said to her.

She looked at me blankly, and I nudged her with my elbow as I stood up. She stood and scowled at me. "That was my best trick, Rebekah. What do you want to leave for?"

"C'mon," I whispered huskily.

We went down to the activity room, but after a while I figured Mildred was ready for some comfort from a friend. So I came up, glad that I hadn't passed her mother on her way out. No amount of sympathy from me seemed to cheer her up, though, and the next day in school her resistance to insults was lower than usual. That was the day she got accused of having head lice.

"You take that back," I yelled at Kevin

Schultz, this big bully in our class. He had to be fourteen years old and must have stayed back three times.

All Mildred did was cower. It was at recess, and we were in the playground. Kevin gave me a look that was supposed to reduce me to a quivering mass of Jell-O. But because I was sticking up for Mildred, I had twice my usual courage. So I stared him down and yelled again, "You heard me. Take that back!"

"Why should I?" he glowered at me as he came closer.

He was at least a head taller than I was. So I knew the only way I could fight him was dirty. I kept my eyes on his so he wouldn't look away, left my arms limp at my sides so he wouldn't think I was starting anything, and then kicked him on his shin as hard as I could.

It worked. It took him completely off guard. He doubled up and grabbed his leg. That gave me an advantage. I brought my arm up under his jaw, and my fist landed with a good crack. Then he pulled himself together, stood up straight, made a fist of his own and hit me on the front of my shoulder. That forced me against the side of the building. I bounced back toward him as if I'd been on a trampoline and started punching him with both my fists wherever I could.

A gang of kids gathered, and one of the girls gasped, "Ooh, he'll kill her."

Not if I kill him first, I thought, and let go with another swift kick to his shin.

I felt a strong hand squeeze my arm. It came from behind me, so I knew it didn't belong to the kid I was hitting.

"Both of you will come with me to the principal's office."

It was a teacher with an unfriendly voice, and I had a gut feeling that the conference in the principal's office wasn't going to turn out in my favor.

Mildred was standing by the doorway looking like death would be welcome. I wanted to console her somehow, but there was no possible way to do it with the teacher practically pushing me into the room.

Mr. Goodwin was sitting at his desk, leaning his elbows on it with his fingers interlaced. He looked at us like a judge in court.

First he started with the bully. "That's not the sort of behavior I would expect from you, Kevin."

From my knowledge of Kevin, it was exactly what *I* would expect.

"And Rebekah!" Mr. Goodwin looked at me with such surprise you'd think that I'd come from the best family in Meacham County and had suddenly committed assault with a dangerous weapon. "Is that what they teach you at the Little Wanderers?"

I know there was real loathing in the look I gave him. Sure that's what they teach us. Fight for your own survival. They don't teach it to you directly though. It's something you pick up from the way they treat you. I don't know how people like Kevin learn the same thing, seeing as how they come from whole, loving families.

Goodwin shook his head. It was obvious he felt that fighting was "unladylike." It's okay for boys, I wanted to shout at him, and okay if boys pick on girls who are smaller and easily hurt by crude remarks. That's okay, isn't it?

I didn't listen to another word out of Goodwin. I knew I wasn't missing anything worth listening to.

"Rebekah, you shouldn't have." Mildred looked at me with her sad brown eyes after we got out of our last class.

"Course I should have, Mildred. If he opens his ugly mouth again, I'll break his face. He can't talk that way to you."

"Rebekah, that was more than—I mean—well, I don't think you ought to. . . ." Her voice dwindled to almost nothing.

"Don't you worry, Mildred. I think he knows who's in charge now."

Her lip twitched slightly as she went into the library for some afterschool work, and I watched her, thinking, if I didn't look after her she'd be in real bad trouble.

Later, not half an hour after I got back to my dorm, Baker's voice sounded from the P.A. system in the hall. "Rebekah Blount, report to Miss Crane's office."

Miss Crane was the counselor for Building A.

If she summoned me, it meant that Goodwin had sent over a formal complaint. There were only three of the kids in my dorm at the time. Allie and Marie looked panicky and Madelaine sounded worse. "Where can they send you from here?" The only thing that made it bearable was that Mildred wasn't there.

Miss Crane is around thirty, and I used to think she had a potential for understanding. But when I got into her office, I could tell that Meacham was getting to her.

"Rebekah, I'm so disappointed in you."

That, in my opinion, is the wrong way to start a conversation with someone you want to inspire to better things. I just looked at her desk.

"Sit down, Rebekah."

I sat.

"Mr. Goodwin told me all about the scene in the playground."

"How could he? He wasn't there." I lifted my eyes to her face.

"The teacher described it to him as she saw it." Miss Crane was patient.

"She didn't know what made it happen."

"What made it happen?"

I shrugged. "It doesn't matter. But you can believe me, that bully Kevin was wrong."

"Tell me about it, Rebekah."

I wasn't going to. Who would believe that I'd start a fight with a boy maybe three years older than me because I was defending some other kid? I wouldn't even try. I hadn't with Goodwin either, because I knew he'd think I was making the whole thing up to save my own skin.

Miss Crane sighed. "You know this sort of thing gives Meacham a bad image in the community."

Crane was now making me responsible for the rotten reputation that rotten orphanage had. I gave her a cold eye.

"Well," she said in a last-resort tone, "your behavior doesn't help to qualify you for acceptance in anybody's home, foster or otherwise."

The "otherwise" part made my throat feel blocked with pebbles. Well, I hadn't had such high hopes before this anyhow, so I really hadn't lost anything.

That all happened in June. School let out, and during the summer Meacham has an arrangement with different families to take kids for a week or two at a time. That was okay—it was like a vacation. The couple I got to go with had a cottage at the beach, and I helped take care of their baby. For that short a time it was easy not to get attached to the people.

The weekend I got back, a lot of prospective parents were there looking around for kids. Since I knew I wasn't being considered, I managed to stay clear of any visitors. No sense in eating my heart out. They usually hung around the playground and athletic fields so they could "observe." It was pitiful the way some kids would act in front of grown-ups. They'd flash their best smiles and do everything but sit up and beg.

It was a hot and muggy day, so I didn't mind staying indoors. I was alone in my dorm, reading. It was a terrific book called *Onion John* about a guy who was sort of the town nut and a kid who thought his father was the most perfect man in the world. I liked to pretend that my father would have been like that—perfect. But it was only pretending. Mine couldn't have been perfect if he never came to see me. I was at a place in the story where I was close to getting weepy and was glad no one was there to see me when Baker's voice came through the P.A. again.

"Rebekah Blount, report to Miss Crane's office."

Oh God, what had I done now? The people I was with for the past two weeks seemed to like me, and I had no reason to think they'd said anything bad. I'd been back less than twenty-four hours, seven of which I'd spent sleeping, and I had no recollection of any laws I'd broken during the sixteen I was awake.

Miss Crane's door was open and I heard voices.

"Yes, she's exactly the right age," a man's voice said.

Was she talking to the police? Was I just the right age to be sent to a reform school and they were sending me because—well, I couldn't figure out any becauses. Was it just a whim of Baker's to get rid of me? What was happening? It was my life—didn't I have any rights at all?

CHAPTER 3

"Oh there you are, Rebekah." Miss Crane said it as if she'd been searching the whole county for me.

My eyes strayed over to the side of the room to the somebody who was connected to the other voice.

There were two people. A lady and a man, probably in their thirties, and they were sitting on the two chairs that filled up all the rest of the space in Miss Crane's office.

"Rebekah, I'd like you to meet Mr. and Mrs. Lawrence. They're looking for a nice twelve-year-old girl to take on a picnic this afternoon. I thought you'd be just the one to fill the bill. What do you say?"

Hypocrite, is what I thought, but I didn't say it out loud. These people must want a foster child. The last time she had talked to me privately, she had acted as if I were going to be put on her never-never list. What happened that made her call *me?* She must not like the Lawrences. Well, I wasn't going to like them either or let them like me because I wasn't going to get borrowed again, then have grief when I had to leave.

21

I looked at Miss Crane without any particular expression of happiness about going picnicking and deliberately avoided looking at Mr. and Mrs. Lawrence. That would give them a chance to change their mind.

"To be perfectly honest, Rebekah, I wanted a twelve-year-old boy, but Rosemary here insisted on a girl, and I'm being a good sport about it."

I turned and looked at Mr. Lawrence, who was standing now with his hands dug all the way down into his bleached-out jeans' pockets. You'd think a crack like that would burn me up. But he didn't say it like a crack. He was smiling with his whole face, and the smile made indentations all along his cheeks. I liked his looks and was annoyed with myself for that reaction. Who cared if he was nice or if he looked like Paul Newman? This was probably his be-kind-to-orphan-girls Saturday, and there was no question in my mind that he would prefer throwing a football around with a boy to picnicking with me.

"Tom doesn't know what fun a picnic can be. Let's show him, Rebekah."

It would have been easy for me to smile at both of them and show some enthusiasm, but I caught myself in time. No sense being taken in by good looks and a sense of humor.

"Okay, you'll have to prove it to me." Tom filled in the silence I had made by not answering Rosemary.

Rosemary stood up and said, acting as if she

hadn't noticed I still hadn't talked, "We'll take you on, Tom Lawrence." She reached out her arm to take mine and smiled, "Let's go!"

They sure must be desperate for a kid, was all I could think. I certainly didn't give them any encouragement for all that friendliness.

"That sounds like a challenge you can't refuse." Miss Crane was gushy. I figured she must have a quota of people she has to match up with kids in order to keep her job.

Then, like that was their cue, the Lawrences sort of swooped me up, and the three of us left the building. At the picnic grounds there were swarms of other people all ages, with balls and kites and a lot of action. In general, I remember Rosemary and Tom being casual and my feeling comfortable with them. Rosemary and I ganged up on Tom, playing tag, Frisbee, and a game of catch with the football they had brought along. At the end we all flopped down on the grass, and Rosemary said to me, "Since he lost, shall we give him any barbecued chicken?"

"Hey, *I* made that chicken. What gives?"

"Well, I'm in charge of serving it. Do we share it with him, Rebekah?"

She winked at me. I remember that part clearly because it struck me then that no grown-up had ever done that to me before. Not that particular thing, I mean, but what it meant—like something just between the two of us.

Then she opened the picnic basket. When I

saw how everything was laid out, with colored paper plates, cups, and napkins—it made me think I was at a banquet. There was potato salad, coleslaw, two different kinds of soft drinks, and a chocolate cake that was feathery heaven.

"Rebekah," Tom sighed with the ecstasy I was feeling when we were both full, "if you'll come to a picnic every week, I'll promise to barbecue whatever you like, and you can name the desserts too. Rosemary is pretty good in that department."

Every week? The idea of being with them every single week gave me chills from my shoulders to my heels. Having that to look forward to would keep me going Sunday through Friday.

What was I thinking? I wasn't going to get myself involved in any more temporary, short-term relationships. Don't weaken, Rebekah, I warned myself.

I wondered why they were having a foster child at all. Maybe it was just for the summer, while their own child or children were away at summer camp and they were lonesome.

"It doesn't have to be a picnic. Maybe you'd rather visit us at home?"

I was scared. I'd better quit this with them right now. I looked at Tom but didn't give him an answer.

"Well, you can think about it. We'll call Miss Crane."

I shook my head up and down, like a marionette being pulled by strings. Why was I saying yes?

It was after five o'clock when we got back to Building A. Miss Crane was gone, so we had to find Baker because I had to be checked in.

"I'll see if she's in her room," I said, moving toward the stairway.

"I just saw her talking with someone by the basketball court," Tom said. "I'll tell her we delivered you safe and sound." Those indentations showed again on his face.

Rosemary leaned toward me, then stopped. Then she quickly leaned forward again and put a smack on my cheek. My heart thumped. "I hope we see you next week." She gave me a little smile and gently squeezed my arm.

I must have said good-bye. I remember standing in the same spot even after they were out of sight, looking into the distance and having strange feelings all over me.

Sunday, the local Rotarians sponsored their annual noble deed and took a bunch of us to a lake for an outing. They had races and games; we swam and had hot dogs for lunch and were supposed to look happy all afternoon. We managed. I mean it wasn't bad, really. I guess it was only that it was so impersonal. People were friendly, but you didn't even know the names of the grown-ups who were trying to be nice. It wasn't that we'd ever see them again, even. And some brought their own kids along. They always did that so we could feel like one big family. It never works. Their kids bend over backwards to do the right thing, but everyone feels clumsy.

Monday and Tuesday were mostly just hanging-around days. There were some sports activities that I made a pass at, and the carpentry room was open, but that didn't appeal to me.

I kept thinking of the Lawrences. I mean, I wondered about them. Did they have any kids, and how come they wanted a twelve-year-old to take out, boy *or* girl? In between all that I was upset about Kathy because she cried a lot for no special reason, and on top of that, Mildred was moping around. She had a reason, though. She had gotten a letter from her mother, which she stroked as if it were a puppy. The letter came instead of a visit.

"Maybe she'll be able to make it next—uh—month." I wasn't sure that that lame encouragement was going to cheer her up any, but I wanted to give her *something* to look forward to. Or let her know I cared, anyway.

"She'll try to, I know she will," she answered.

Wednesday, Mildred and I decided we'd go see if any bikes were available for us to ride, and as we passed her office, Miss Crane called to us.

"Rebekah, I just spoke with Mrs. Lawrence on the phone. She said that if you were free next Saturday, she and her husband would like you to go with them to the beach."

My head started to pound. Sure I'd like to go. And free was what I was. "I. . . ." I opened my mouth to tell her yes. But then I clamped it shut. I'd rather stick around here, even if the temperature got up to 95, with humidity to match. Nobody was going to dangle something in front of me that I couldn't have for keeps. No thanks. Besides, how could I accept while Mildred had nowhere to go?

"And Mildred," Miss Crane turned to her, "you know your visit with the Hennings starts Saturday. Remember?"

"Oh, yes," she nodded, smiling, "I'd forgotten that."

"Well, that makes it just fine for the two of you. The Lawrences want to get an early start—about 9:30."

That seemed to settle it for me, regardless of my resolutions. Well, all right, I'd go this time. At least Mildred was taken care of. But I was going to remember to keep a good hold on myself. No matter how much fun I was having—no matter how kind, loving, or generous those people were—I'd keep telling myself over and over that I was a summer fill-in for them, and come fall they'd forget they ever met me.

CHAPTER 4

I hated myself for letting it happen. It was a perfect day, probably the best in my life, and I let them know it. How dumb could I get, I thought to myself. I had let all my defenses down, and it would take me at least a month to build them up again.

I remembered how I used to be so disgusted over the way the kids acted on visiting days so they'd get picked. But I wasn't acting! It wasn't enough that I told Rosemary and Tom, "Thank you" at least two hundred and fifty times. I made it worse by saying, "Oh, I hope I see you again." The payoff was when I said, sounding like I was real envious, "Your children sure are lucky."

They gave each other a quick, just-between-the-two-of-us look, and Rosemary said, "We don't have any children."

"Oh." I was surprised. It was a good thing I didn't add, "Boy, with such nice people like you, that's a terrible loss."

"But we're very fond of kids, Rebekah, don't think we're not," Tom said, and I said, "You must be." I tried to get across that I didn't think they took me out to punish themselves.

Then, after they brought me back and Tom said, "I know Rosemary would like to see your dorm, Becky," that did it. I mean it was like I belonged to them, calling me Becky like that. It all went to my head and softened whatever fraction of a brain I had left. So instead of coming out of the clouds and saying to Rosemary, "My dorm is terrific along with everything else here and quit leading me down a dead-end street," I started apologizing for the dorm, as if I wanted her to pity me and take me in as her foster child that very minute.

"The dorm isn't much," I mumbled as we walked up the stairs.

"What makes a room much?" she challenged me.

"Well it doesn't have—I mean it's not. . . ." I was ready to spill out that it wasn't like a bedroom in someone's house. But that would have made it sound like I was wide open for takers.

"Doesn't have Persian rugs? Fancy furniture?" She put her arm around my shoulders and drew me close to her. "I didn't expect it to be the palace at Versailles." She looked down into my face as we got to the landing. It's a wonder I didn't break down and carry on like Mildred's mother.

We got to my doorway, and I gave the room a fast once-over glance. Sure it was no Versailles palace, but it didn't have that lived-in look either that I'd seen in private homes. Real bedrooms get that look from stuffed animals or fancy pillows, or maybe a record player, posters, or just personal stuff lying around. But this dorm, like the rest of the dorms at Meacham, looked like a hospital ward. Seven beds all in a row, with white bedspreads and nothing on them to break the monotony.

Allie was the only one there. She was standing by a window, looking out. Madelaine, Marie, and Mary Ellen were away with families, and Kathy was most likely getting therapy at the moment. I felt strange, coming in with Rosemary, and Allie all alone. Should I introduce them or not?

"How nice to have friends to share a room with," Rosemary said suddenly, loud enough for Allie to hear. "I was an only child, and I hardly ever had anyone sleep over. I missed that."

Simple and easy, just like that she made it right.

"Listen, if we didn't have each other to talk to we'd go bananas, wouldn't we, Allie?" I called over to her. She had to turn around, and it broke the ice.

Allie warmed up to Rosemary, and we had this three-way give and take for a few minutes. Nothing earthshaking, just nice. Then Rosemary said, "Tom's probably trying to decide if he should go home without me. I'm not going to let him do that." Then she said to Allie, "I hope I see you again real soon." Allie broke out in this big grin. "Sure hope so."

Rosemary didn't give me a kiss or hug on her

way out. I knew she would have if Allie hadn't been there. I mean I knew Rosemary had sensitivity. She wouldn't hurt someone else's feelings by making them feel left out. So at the door she said to me, "Next week?" It was almost more a statement of fact than a question. As if we'd already made the date.

I was practically getting cramps in my stomach thinking about it, knowing I was getting close to loving her and Tom and knowing how it was all going to end.

"Gee, she's neat," Allie said admiringly.

"Yeah, she is." I didn't look at her.

"Is she going to be your next foster mother?"

Allie asked it innocently enough, but it was like she'd stuck a dagger or something right in my middle. I closed my eyes and shook my head hard, all the way, from shoulder to shoulder.

"Well, what is she taking you out for? Is there something wrong? I thought she seemed to like you, Rebekah."

"What's the point?"

"What do you mean?"

"I mean I'm not moving out of here to go into one more foster home unless I absolutely hate the people!"

"You crazy?"

"Well, then it won't matter!"

"You're crazy."

"Well, do *you* like going from house to house and family to family and then when you get to feel you're part of them they send you *back?*"

"Course not! But it's better than staying here!"

"I'm not so sure of that. You *like* starting in with new schools every time you get fostered out and trying to get in with new kids?"

"No, but it's still better than staying here," she repeated.

I'd never seen Allie so agitated before.

"Well, my memory must be better than yours, Allie." I remembered the hassles I'd had.

"You just move around here?"

I used to swallow hard, pretty sure how the rest of it was going to go. Actually it could go two ways. Either,

"Where do you live?"

And I'd say, "42 Taylor Street."

Then someone would say, "42 Taylor? That's where the Careys live. Oh, you must be their new foster child." And that would destroy me.

Or, "What's your name?"

"Rebekah Blount."

"Where do you live?"

"42 Taylor."

"42 Taylor? Oh, the Careys must have moved."

And I'd know the Careys hadn't moved because the Careys were my new foster parents, and I hadn't gotten around to remembering I was supposed to use their name instead of mine.

Allie and I didn't settle anything that day. We still kept the same ideas we started with, and all week I tried getting involved in whatever program was listed on the bulletin board in the activity room. I could have made the *Guinness Book of World Records* for starting and quitting more projects in a five-day period than anyone in the world. Monday I tried needlepoint, and after half an hour I decided it was the most boring thing ever invented. Tuesday I tried the painting class and came to the same conclusion. Wednesday I joined a group going to the Natural History Museum and that night had a nightmare about skeletons. Thursday we went to the zoo, and that was worse, since I imagined I could see all the bones in the animals. On Friday I sat through a children's concert in the park, but my mind wandered even in the middle of Tschaikovsky's *Nutcracker Suite*. Considering the whole week, if I'd been graded on Decision-Making Skills, I would have flunked the course.

I knew what the trouble was, too. I had an important decision to make, and it wasn't going to be easy.

Rosemary or Tom would be calling for me to go out with them again on Saturday. Was I going to let myself get in deeper? They had to be leading up to fostering me. They probably already filled out an application form. Any time now I'd be told about it.

It was Friday afternoon, and I was walking past Miss Crane's office. She was getting ready to leave.

"Hi, Rebekah. I hope you have a nice weekend."

Now she was going to tell me they called.

"Thanks." I smiled at her. I could at least pretend I was going to like what she'd tell me.

"See you Monday," she said, going toward the front door on her way out.

Nobody called me? Well, that's good, I said to myself. Very good. Now that's settled and I don't have to worry about making a decision.

Around eight o'clock that night, when I started up the stairs, it suddenly struck me. They didn't call! They don't want me! Why don't they want me! They *have* to want me!

What was I thinking? I'm supposed to be relieved. That's one family I won't have any heartaches over leaving because I'm not going there in the first place. I'm never going anywhere. Nobody ever wanted me. What's wrong with people anyway? Why do flesh-and-blood parents give up their own kids? Other people don't want secondhand children.

"Rebekah Blount, how many times do you have to be called? You're wanted on the telephone."

That was Baker's angry voice sounding from the bottom of the stairs. I was standing on the landing without any recollection of how I'd gotten there. All I remembered was moving up a couple of steps and then getting lost in thought about how rotten the world was.

"Oh, I'm sorry, Miss Baker. I didn't hear you."

"Well, you're keeping Mr. Lawrence waiting." Her eyes bored into me. "You can take it in Miss Crane's office."

By some miracle, Baker had the decency to wait in the hall while I walked in a daze to the telephone.

"H—H—Hello?" I know it didn't sound like me.

"Becky? Is that you Becky?"

"Oh, Tom! Tom, I thought you forgot." That was all. And then, while he was telling me that he would pick me up at nine sharp the next morning, my eyes got blurred and the tears fell. I didn't even try to stop them or wipe them away.

CHAPTER 5

It was like a fairy tale. Okay, I know that sounds silly, but it's the truth.

Tom came at nine o'clock, and he was his usual smiley self, but you could tell he had something on his mind besides just taking me out for the day. As soon as he started the car, he said, looking straight out the windshield, "Before we go to the beach, Rosemary and I want to talk to you about an important matter."

He means they're going to tell me they want to foster me. I'll let them, I thought, feeling happy and helpless at the same time. It's just more than I can handle, and I'm not going to fight it any more. When the time comes that they give me up, I'll have to bear it, but I want to live with them so much now that I don't care—I won't even think about the future.

"Let's wait to talk about it until we see Rosemary," he said.

I said, "Sure."

Tom brought up at least five different subjects for conversation, none of which had anything to do with what we were really most interested in right then. For the whole ride I felt like a tightrope walker holding raw eggs inside their shells in each hand. Then when Rosemary opened the door of their apartment and I could see she looked nervous, I felt like I'd dropped the eggs.

I said "Hi," but Rosemary just took my hand and swallowed hard. I thought, boy, I won't be able to stand *this* much longer. In another second I'll have to shout "Okay, already. I'll be your foster child." Of course it never occurred to me that that wasn't what they had in mind.

They led me over to their gold-colored sofa, and the three of us sat down. We were very tense and not at all like how we'd been up till then. They were on either side of me, clearing their throats and exchanging looks with each other and then with me. I was sitting very straight but was still aware of how luxurious the sofa felt.

Rosemary said "Rebekah" and Tom said "Becky" at the same time. I giggled nervously, and all at once Rosemary got in control of herself and seemed very sure of what she had to say.

"Rebekah," her face was close to mine and her eyes had such a loving look in them it made me want to cry, "we want to adopt you."

Adopt! I could hardly form the word in my mind.

"We've been thinking about this for a long time, you know," she went on, in a way so that I would know this was no light thing with them. "We hope you feel the same."

I put my hand up to my head. I felt a little dizzy and *very* strange.

Then Tom got up and stood in front of me. "Now listen, Becky," he said, being very serious. "To be perfectly frank, I had wanted a twelve-year-old boy. But you know what?" He cupped my chin in his hand and tilted my head up, so I had to look straight at him. "I've decided I want you, that's what." Then he bent over and kissed me.

It was a funny thing. All the time—all those years—I'd been hoping, giving up hope, and hoping again that I'd get picked for adoption, I used to think that if it happened I'd jump up and down, run around like a nut, and scream with joy. But now I was *there*—and I was numb.

Being numb, of course, doesn't mean you're in a coma. You're aware of what's going on, and it's quite possible to have total recall of the situation afterward. I think that except for a few inconsequential items, I could tell in detail everything that happened from that minute until now, almost a year later.

The thing that stands out in my mind over all the others isn't so much what we said and did right then, but the scene at Meacham when I was leaving. I was supposed to be wildly happy. After all, wasn't that what I'd been praying for as far back as I could remember? In bed at night, after lights out, hadn't I begged with every single fiber of my body and every cell in my brain to get out of Meacham and into a family that loved me like the Lawrences did?

And if a miracle happened and you did get adopted, weren't you supposed to tell it to your friends in the happiest, most excited way? I mean you were being transported from prison to paradise.

But that night in the dorm, when everyone was back from their so-called vacations, I found myself feeling only one thing—guilt—as if I'd done something terribly wrong.

"You know th—the—L—Lawrences? Uh, those people who've been taking me out?"

"They're going to be your foster parents! I knew it!" Allie clasped her hands together, pleased at how smart she was.

Now I'd have to tell them it was for adoption. I kept feeling more and more as if I'd made this big goof, and now it was time for a confession. I finally managed to get the words out and waited almost fearfully for congratulations that they didn't feel, jealous cracks, or just silence. What I got made me feel worse. You'd think *they* were the ones who were going, they were so glad.

"Where do they live?"

"Hillcrest."

"Oooh, then they're rich."

"I guess so."

"When are you going?"

"Tomorrow morning."

"Wow, that's fast."

"Are there any other children in the family?"

I could answer that one from what Rosemary and Tom had told me that day.

"No other children. Rosemary was concentrating on her career—she's an architect, Tom's in real estate—and then when they decided they wanted someone, they knew they didn't want it to be a baby."

"Oh, boy, do they have any friends who feel the same way?" Mary Ellen leaned over and gave me an eager look.

"I'll keep my eyes open," I told her, beginning to feel better.

"How come they don't want a baby? Everyone wants to adopt a baby."

"Well," I explained, "they've been married almost fourteen years, and they figured if they had a baby right off, it would have been around twelve now."

"Ooh, you're so lucky."

There were whispers that night long after the lights were out, until we were sure Bigfoot was on her way into our room.

Sunday morning, the whole atmosphere was different. Like the real fact suddenly hit them all. They weren't going anywhere—I was.

Allie talked about God knows who'd sleep in my bed, and Marie said since Baker would have one less to pick on she'd probably get tougher on the rest. Madelaine complained that nobody except me ever watched her new card tricks, and Mary Ellen reminded me, like a threat, "You better find out if they have any friends interested in half-grown girls."

I couldn't even think of one joke to make about any of it.

Then Kathy hugged me hard, and it was tough pulling myself away from her. I walked to the door carrying my old cloth suitcase and turned around for one last look. Mildred hadn't said good-bye yet. I think I must have deliberately been avoiding her. How could I just walk out on the one person who needed me more than any of the others? A sharp pain in my head was letting me know I couldn't ignore her.

She was standing by the window—the same one Allie had been looking out of when I came in with Rosemary the week before. Mildred was my best friend, and she was stuck here. She wasn't getting released for adoption, and she wasn't going home. And there'd be nobody to stand up for her if she got accused of having head lice. She turned to face me, and her pitiful and lonely expression increased my pain.

I dropped my bag and ran to her, crying out, "Oh Mildred, I don't want to go!"

But Mildred, poor, pitiful Mildred, grabbed me by my shoulders and squeezed me hard. "Yes you do, Rebekah! Nobody is ever going to call you a Little Wanderer again!"

CHAPTER 6

I've come to realize how easy it is for a person to get corrupted. That's a pretty strong word, and I'm not thinking of it in the sense of something immoral. What I mean is, sometimes no matter how sincere your intentions are, if something very tempting gets in the way, all your sincerity can go down the drain.

Not that I'm apologizing for my actions. But I'm not proud of myself either. I guess I'm just explaining.

I walked out of my dorm room that Sunday trying to blink back the tears. I knew I couldn't let Mildred down by carrying on, so I got myself out of there dry-eyed to where Rosemary and Tom were waiting in their car in front of Building A.

It crossed my mind as I saw their faces that when they saw me walk through that door they must have felt the way parents do when they take their baby home from the hospital after it's born. I got a sinking feeling that I wasn't worthy of their love, but at the same time I made a strong resolve to live up to their expectations. If you've ever been in a situation where there's a contradiction like that you know it isn't easy. There was the additional complication of my feeling like a deserter, walking out on the kids.

Going down the stairs I had said, "I'll never forget them," moving my lips soundlessly. Before I opened the outside door, I stood there for a few seconds, just long enough to say it again. "I'll never forget them!"

From Meacham to the Lawrences' is about a twenty-minute drive, but the areas are so different they could be light-years away from each other. The Home was built a century ago, when the whole area was out in the country. Now it's all changed. The trees have been cut down, bus stops are out front, gas stations are on two corners, and a superhighway is a block away. Meacham's buildings, surrounded by a high iron fence, look out of place—almost like they think they're still out in the country and won't join the neighborhood they're in the middle of.

Ten Oakwood Circle, my new address, was a high-rise of glass, brick, and natural wood—the kind of place that some people refer to as posh. There's another building, its twin, across the circle, and in between them and at each end are gardens with clipped lawns that look like thick velvet. The minute your car turns into Hillcrest—that's the name of the section—you know you're in a pretty ritzy place. Unless you're jogging, you're not on foot in Hillcrest. Even though there are sidewalks, they're skinny and three-quarters covered with moss, all of which means they're not meant to be walked on. In Oakwood Circle you rarely see a whole human form, since the tenants drive in and out through an underground garage. Outside the circle, everyone lives in private houses in Hillcrest. Tom said the natives raised a big fuss over the apartments going up, and the Board of Aldermen discussed it for months before they finally let it happen. The compromise was on the height of the building—nine floors. We're on the ninth. The view is exceptional. So is my room.

"Rebekah, we've used this just as an extra room, and I purposely didn't get any real bedroom furniture until. . . ." She gave me an extra wide smile. "We can pick it out together, okay?"

What could be wrong with that? Nothing. The room was beautiful, and with no effort at all you could let the picture of seven drab beds in a row in an orphanage dormitory fall out of your mind.

And who could remember Christy's cooking with the meals Rosemary and Tom prepared? They were artists with food. Through them I found out that there are greater tastes in the world than hamburgers and pizza. I already knew about Tom's barbecued chicken.

The terrible thing was that even that very first night, which was weeks before I'd even pick out my new bedroom set, I fell blissfully to sleep without one solitary thought of my friends—friends that I had sworn only a few hours earlier never to forget.

"Sweetie, what do you think about these curtains?"

"Would you like wall-to-wall carpeting or Solarium tile and some throw rugs?"

"Becky, tomorrow we'll get you roller skates . . . and a bike. I think a ten-speed would be the best."

It went on like that for the rest of the summer.

It took me three weeks to get around to it. Then I asked Rosemary if I could call the kids on the phone.

"Of course, sweetie. And if you'd like, ask them to come with us to the beach tomorrow."

Phone calls aren't the easiest things to put through at my former residence. First of all, the line is always busy. Then when you finally get connected, they have to ring Miss Crane's extension, and you're lucky if she's not on it. Also, you have to make your calls during Miss Crane's working hours unless it's an emergency. Then Baker answers, and that I'd just as soon skip.

"Rebekah? Is that you Rebekah?" Miss Crane recognized my voice.

I don't know why that should have surprised me. I'd talked to her often enough.

"How are you doing?" She sounded really interested. I don't know why that surprised me either.

"Fine. Just fine," I said. I hoped she didn't think that was just an expression. After all, she was the one who made the adoption arrangements for me.

"I'm glad, Rebekah. They're good people."

"I know."

"Was there something. . . . ?"

"Oh . . . Oh, yeah—could I speak with Mildred? I—uh—just want to say hello."

"Sure thing, Rebekah. Nice talking to you."

"Same here."

I heard her through the P.A. system. "Mildred Watson—telephone."

I hoped that didn't scare Mildred, but it was better than getting the message through Baker. Then it was quiet, and it seemed like an hour and I wondered if we got cut off. Then I heard a wobbly "Hello." My heart fluttered. It was strange using a telephone to talk to Mildred. The only times we had been separated in the four years since she'd been at Meacham was when we were in foster homes. So hearing her voice on the phone, I felt like you do sometimes when you've eaten too much. You know, that heavy, sick sensation right under your ribs.

"Mildred it's me, Rebekah. How are you? I mean—what—what's new?"

It was so stupid, acting as if we hardly knew each other.

"Oh Rebekah! Is it like you thought, Rebekah? It must be great, right?"

Oh God, how could I even answer her?

"It's . . . okay . . . real good, I mean." She'd

think from that it was rotten, and that I was putting up a brave front. Now no matter what I said, it wasn't going to come out right.

"See, I told you." She said it the way you'd comfort a little kid when he stopped crying after falling down. "I told you it wasn't going to hurt, didn't I?" You know, reassuring.

It honestly gave me a kind of weird feeling. Up to the time I left Meacham, Mildred was the one who got comforted. I did the comforting. Now she was doing it, as if I was getting picked on.

"Mildred, we're going to the beach tomorrow. Rosemary said it'd be okay for all the kids to come. Do you think you could?"

There was a wailing sound on the other end of the phone.

"What's the matter?"

"Oh Rebekah. Does it have to be tomorrow? I mean I can't go tomorrow. I just *can't*. My *mother* is coming."

For more than two months her mother had been among the missing, and then the one day Mildred gets an invitation to go to the beach her mother decides to show. I didn't want anyone else if Mildred couldn't come. I liked all the kids—it wasn't that. But I figured that even though she was going to have her mother with her, she'd be left out of having a good time with us, and I didn't want her to miss that. I wasn't 100 percent convinced that having her mother there was such a big treat, either.

So what I said was, "Mildred, guess what? They're giving the weather report on the radio, and the weatherman just said rain for Saturday. So we probably won't go to the beach anyway."

That didn't make me a hero though. Because I was sore that Mildred's mother was coming, I cheated five other kids out of a decent day away from Meacham.

CHAPTER 7

I was pretty busy the rest of the summer. Not only getting clothes and stuff for my room, but Rosemary and Tom took a lot of days off from work, and the three of us went places. The best was overnight camping in state parks, where we slept in sleeping bags and cooked outdoors and hiked the trails. I used my new ten-speed a lot. It was really neat riding with Rosemary and Tom. Sometimes, as soon as it got light, we'd go out for an hour or so, then come back to our campsite and fix breakfast. I didn't even miss not knowing anyone my own age.

I suppose you think it's strange that a girl who spent almost all her whole life in a County Home could move in with people from another world, from the other side of the tracks you could say, and have it turn out like a blend of milk and honey. But I honestly think, looking back on it, that some things must be prearranged, like made in heaven.

Oh, there were some rough spots. Like one afternoon while we were camping, we'd just come back from a bird-watching walk—that's Tom's hobby —and I felt like looking at the waterfalls around the bend from our tent. Naturally, I asked permission to go. After all, at Meacham you barely took a breath without asking.

"Okay if I go down to the river, Rosemary? I won't stay long."

"Of course." She said it offhandedly, almost like she didn't think I even had to ask.

Before I started off, I saw Tom give her a hard stare. I couldn't figure out why, and as soon as he thought I was past hearing distance, which I wasn't, he said, "Why did you let her go down there alone?"

"What do you mean *let* her? She's twelve years old, Tom."

"She's too young to go off on her own, especially in a strange place. She could drown, for gosh sakes!" He sounded angry.

I just stood there. This was the first time I'd heard them have a disagreement. And it was on account of me. I didn't know whether to run back and apologize or just keep standing there listening. I didn't do either one. I started to run and didn't stop until I got to the bank of the river. I stayed there for what seemed like a long time, just looking at the water. In the foster homes I'd been in, if there were ever any arguments between the people, it didn't matter to me. But this was different. Rosemary and Tom were special, and I didn't want anything to change. Maybe I shouldn't get in too deep with them after all, I thought, because if it doesn't work out I'll get hurt again. Didn't I remember what happened with Marie? She was that close to getting adopted, and then the couple got a divorce and neither one of them wanted her and she got shipped right back to Meacham. That could happen to me, couldn't it?

When I finally got back to our campsite, everything seemed okay. I mean, there was no yelling going on, so they must have settled it between them. But neither one said anything about it to me.

Something else came up soon after we got back to the city. Up till that particular night, Rosemary and Tom hadn't gone out without me. They had some friends over, and a few times the three of us went out to a restaurant together. But this one night they were invited to a dinner party—adults only, naturally.

When Rosemary got the telephone call about it I happened to be sitting opposite her at the kitchen table.

"Sure, Pam," she said into the mouthpiece. "We'd love to—Oh!" As soon as she said, "Oh," she put her hand over her mouth, looked at me, looked away, then dropped her hand and said "Oh" again. "We can't, Pam. I mean, how can we?"

Then Tom came in the room. He raised his eyebrows in a "What's up?" expression, and Rosemary told Pam she'd have to let her know and hung up.

"Let her know what?" Tom asked.

Rosemary seemed uncomfortable, as if she

wished Tom hadn't asked. "She wants to know if we can have dinner at their house next Saturday night, but I don't know if we can make it."

"Why not? What have we got on?"

"Oh—er—uh. . . ." Rosemary stood up and carefully set the chair against the table. She seemed to be stalling for time to come up with a good answer. I guessed she didn't want to go to the dinner, which surprised me considering what close friends she and Pam were.

"What's the matter, Rosey?" Tom looked irritated.

"Well," she exhaled a breath you could really hear. "I might as well be frank." She leaned her hands on the top of the chair back.

All I could imagine was that she must have had a fight with her friend Pam. But that wasn't like Rosemary, and besides, she sounded excited about the dinner until she said the first "Oh." Tom had his hands dug in his pockets, waiting.

"I don't think it's right to leave Rebekah alone."

I nearly fell off my chair.

Tom was shocked too. "You're kidding."

"No, I'm not." She put the emphasis on the "not," as if she were trying to defend her opinion.

I opened my mouth to tell her that I didn't need a baby-sitter, but Tom got to her before me. He raised his voice, and it reminded me of the other time they'd had an argument on account of me.

"How come you thought it was all right for her

to be alone at a twenty-foot gushing waterfall but not all right for her to stay in the safety of our ninth-floor apartment with all the security that our monthly rent pays for?"

Why did they have to *do* this? And Tom wasn't even using my name—just saying *she* and *her*. This wasn't the way it was supposed to be. Rosemary looked miserable. "Oh," she said, looking at me, "we're so new at this. We have so much to *learn*."

"Well, I hope we're fast learners," Tom said, and his hand moved, trembling, through his hair. Then he looked over at me. "How are you bearing up, Becky?"

I think all I did was give him a real agonized look.

Rosemary had deep scowl lines between her eyes and she was still clutching the chair back. She looked at me again. "Sweetie, this must be horrible for you too. All I'm trying to say is," and she looked back and forth from me to Tom, "is that I think it's pretty lonely to be in a new place and not know a soul you can spend the evening with while we're off having a good ti—me." Her voice broke on "time," and I flew over to her and hugged her with all my strength.

"Rosemary, I'll be okay—honest I will. I can read or watch TV or—I'll be *okay*." We held each other tight, and when we finally drew apart she shook her head.

"Hey, you're something else."

Tom only said, almost to himself, "Well, praise the Lord."

Then it got to be September, and I was in a frenzy of excitement about my first day at a school with a personal name—the Sarah Margaret Fuller School. I found out afterward that Ms. Fuller had been into women's lib before it was considered all right. She must have been very brave.

Rosemary had spent a lot of lunch hours shopping to get me a wardrobe she felt I wouldn't be ashamed of. But for all the attention anyone paid me, I could just as well have worn rags. What I hadn't counted on was the confusion every one of the seventh-graders, including me, was feeling their very first day in junior high. There was such rushing around you'd think we were all late for a plane, and the yelling was like people getting over six-month cases of laryngitis.

A couple of days later it simmered down, and I got asked, "You new around here?"

My heart did a quick flip-flop. But it wasn't like when I was with the Careys. This time I was going to get adopted. And since there hadn't been any other Lawrence kids, for all anyone knew, I had belonged to them since birth.

It was easy for me to say, "I used to live in District 12."

They accepted that without any more questions about my background. I've found that if there's no special reason to, people don't usually get nosy.

Because I wasn't used to kids at school making me feel I was one of the crowd, I honestly didn't know how to act. Or feel, even. I mean, what if they knew about me? Would they treat me the same? It was hard to know. And that made it hard for me to judge them. Was Terry really as nice as she seemed to be? Should I believe Karen when she said, "I bet you'll be the first girl in the seventh grade to get asked for a date because you're so pretty."

I'd never thought about being pretty, let alone about dates. What was on our minds had been keeping out of Baker's way and getting out of Meacham.

So I did a lot of holding back. I mean, when you've got something in your mind, you can't act free with people—you know, like be real natural. For instance, since I didn't call Rosemary and Tom Mother and Dad, which everyone calls their parents, I had to be careful that I didn't let their first names slip out. I could just imagine the questions I'd get then. So it was like I was on guard.

Rosemary, who is no dummy when it comes to seeing what's going on underneath the surface, gave me a shock when she came right to the point a couple of weeks later.

"You haven't told any of your friends that we're an adoptive family?"

I mumbled, "No," and I was sure she thought I was ashamed of her and Tom. "It's just that," I started to explain but couldn't do it.

"What are you afraid of Rebekah?"

There was no place I could hide from her. I

was squirming inside and couldn't find an answer.

"The principal of Fuller knows. You know that, don't you?"

"Yes."

"Your teachers know," she continued, talking in her gentle way.

"Yes," I said again.

She gave me one of those looks that shoot through the front and come out the back of your skull. I mean, you *know* you've been looked at. And then she said it. "Don't you think the fact that you've been *chosen* counts for anything?"

Oh boy. I felt like two cents, being responsible for a scene like that with her, and a half a cent for not having the guts to come out with the truth. But all I did for an answer was grunt.

"You think the other kids won't like you if you've been adopted?"

"Well, coming from Meacham. . . ." I looked down at the floor. She knew that Meacham wasn't exactly a private school for millionaires' kids.

"Honey, you know you're not being fair to them or to yourself."

"I don't know what you mean."

"You're afraid to have any faith in those girls. That cheats you out of having real friendships."

She was right.

"Don't you think it's more important to find out what those girls are made of? If they don't like you for yourself, then. . . ." The rest of her sentence didn't need finishing.

Inwardly I agreed. But I wasn't ready to put anyone to the test.

CHAPTER 8

I got plenty of chances to put them to the test, that's for sure. They kept being friendly and making me offers.

"C'mon over to my house after school, Rebekah. I've got a new rug in my room. It's one of those furry things in the shape of a foot—you know the kind."

Actually, I didn't know the kind, but I wanted to go. In the neighborhoods I'd been fostered out to before, if I got asked over to anyone's house it wasn't to see anything new they had unless it was a baby.

When Karen said, "Ask your mother if you can come for a sleepover," I came close to fainting. My mother!

With that one word I got shifted back, in my mind, to Meacham. The way I've always looked at it, no matter what the setup was there, the biggest thing we were deprived of was a mother. It might not seem so big a thing to a kid who's always had one, but to me, when certain things happen, I think it's important to have a mother to tell them to.

Like finding out about getting your period. At

Meacham they must have the idea you don't need to have that information until you're twelve years old. I mean they put it off as long as possible. Anyone in our dorm who didn't know sooner found out from Kathy when we were ten. And that, as any girl knows, is late.

Kathy was having problems enough on account of her mother being sick, plus her own fears about herself. Then one morning she woke up screaming. "Ohmygod, I'm gonna die, I'm gonna die, I'm bleeding to death!"

We all sat up in bed, and I ran over to her.

"Where?" I yelled.

She had this terrified expression and was half off her bed with one leg on the floor.

"There!" She pointed to the sheet, her head turned away from it, as if by not looking it would go away.

I could see some bloodstains, nothing like she'd been stabbed or anything, and then it came to me what it was. I had found out about menstruation when I was in the third grade. The older sister of one of the kids in my class had left a box of pads around, and the girl was examining the contents. She was telling her friend about it, and I happened to be standing right there. That gave them the idea to confide in me, only to frighten me I later realized. As a rule, none of us from the Home could be so lucky as to be invited to share any secrets. And the way they described it to me, you'd think there was something abnormal about the whole process. Of course I didn't get it all straight. I mean you never do when you get something second or third hand. I worried about it at first, and afterward I didn't believe it. Then from all the ads I saw and listened to I came out with some half-baked knowledge. But at least I wasn't scared when it happened to Kathy.

"It's only your period, Kathy," I said, trying to calm her.

"What's a period? What do you mean period?" she rattled off hysterically.

"Period!" Madelaine sounded as if she was in shock. "That means you're having a *baby!*"

"Oh—aah—ohh." I thought poor Kathy was going to faint.

"You're not having a baby, Kathy. You're not, you're not!" I was shouting at her.

By this time our whole dorm was standing beside her.

"That's what it means when you bleed like that," Madelaine insisted. "Debby Connor from my last foster home told me that and she was twelve, so she ought to know."

"Well, she didn't know what she was talking about, because all it means is that you *can* have a baby when—when you're grown up. That's what it means," I repeated as if to settle it.

Kathy started shivering, and she still hadn't moved an inch from where we first saw her.

"We better get the nurse."

"What happened?" We all turned toward the doorway where the voices came from. Three girls from another dorm on our floor were bunched together, peering in at us.

Nobody got a chance to explain. Baker was shoving her way through.

I tell you, you haven't seen anything until you've seen Baker first thing in the morning. Ugh. I won't even try to describe her.

"What is all this unnecesary commotion about?"

Every single eye was on her, and I swear we all held our breath. That ugly fink—she didn't know if the commotion was unnecessary or if someone was dying. Before anyone dared open her mouth, Mrs. Ferris, the other housemother in our building, came in.

"Girls, is anything wrong?" Then she spied the big bulk in her brown hairy bathrobe—made of floor sweepings I think. I took an oath that instant that I would never wear any brown bathrobes made of *anything* as long as I lived.

"Oh, Gertrude, I didn't realize you were up. What seems to be the trouble?"

I didn't know why Mrs. Ferris should speak civilly to Baker. She didn't have to like we did.

Baker curled her mouth. "These girls will have to explain what the trouble is. Waking us up at this hour of the morning!"

"This hour of the morning" was exactly six

minutes before the bell that has to get even Baker up. But in the meantime, while she was getting rid of her aggressions, someone could have died. I mean, if it was left to our ignorance about bloodstains, we might have thought it was the end of Kathy. Naturally, Baker didn't care about any of us, including poor, shivering, bloody Kathy.

"You dear child," Mrs. Ferris spotted Kathy and ran to her. "Don't worry dear—it's going to be all right."

See, Mrs. Ferris didn't have to know any details —no more than Baker did. But her attitude was different. It was the way any normal decent human being would have behaved. And Kathy did what anyone in her situation would do, too. She reached out and grabbed Mrs. Ferris around whatever part of Mrs. Ferris was grabbable and held her. Lucky for Kathy it wasn't Baker. She doesn't like to be grabbed—anywhere.

The whole thing ended about twenty minutes after that. Mrs. Ferris sort of took over from there; the nurse checked Kathy out, Baker snorted all the way through breakfast, and everyone went back to their regular routines. And the kids who didn't know about it before got their first knowledge of what getting your period is all about.

But me, I had always dreamed I would some-day get to have those quiet, just-between-the-two-of-us-talks with a mother, about special things that are part of every girl's growing up. And now Rosemary was trying to do that with me, and it was hard for me to let her. I don't think it was anyone's fault. It needed time, that was all.

Of course she let me go to Karen's sleepover, and it was a real super experience. But in the middle of the night when the eight of us were whispering and giggling, I had this awareness, like remembering something in the past that never really happened. When we all finally said good night to each other for the twentieth time, I knew what the memory was. Mildred. We used to do a lot of whispering when the lights were out, but not much giggling went with it. Our not being together now was like it had never really happened at all. I felt so bad about the brand new life I was having, it carried over to the whole next day. Nobody except Rosemary noticed.

"Something went wrong at Karen's?"

"No, not really."

"But *something*."

I just stared into space, like I was lost in thought. She put her arm around me and said, "Don't be upset—whatever it was. Things have a habit of working out."

What could work out? I was living in a real house, part of a real family and meeting new friends, while Mildred was still at Meacham.

"Rosemary, I feel so bad about Mildred." It wasn't easy to say, it hurt so much inside.

"Honey," Rosemary said quietly, "you mustn't

feel you've done something wrong because you're here and she's there."

That didn't help much. I shook my head. All I knew was that if I were with Mildred, it would be better for her.

"Sweetie, her turn will come too."

Would it? And even if it did, no matter how understanding Rosemary was, it didn't change anything that was happening now.

CHAPTER 9

The rule is that you get a six-month trial period before you can legally adopt someone. And three weeks
before that time is up, the state probate court advertises for you on the legal notice page of the newspaper, so that if anyone else wants to claim you, they
can.

"Here it is, Becky." Tom brought the paper
home, folded to the classifieds, the first night the ad
appeared. He read it out loud. "To the parents, parts
unknown, of minor child Rebekah Blount, a petition for adoption of said child has been presented to
Court So and So by the Assistant Commissioner,
Division of Family and Children's Services, etcetera,
praying that the Court establish whether or not your
consent shall be required to said petition for adoption
of said minor child and the name of said child be
changed to Rebekah Lawrence, etcetera, and I love
you and can hardly wait."

"It doesn't say, 'I love you and can hardly wait,
Tom Lawrence!'" Rosemary grabbed the paper.
"Let's have a look at that."

"*It* doesn't say it—*I* say it, and furthermore, I
defy anyone to object!" Tom beamed at us.

I should have beamed back but I couldn't. There wasn't any real good reason for it, but I got scared. The expression on my face must have been different from what Tom thought it would be, because he waited a second and then opened his arms wide to close me in. I felt better, but I wanted to see what that ad looked like in actual print. Rosemary spread the paper on the kitchen table, and we all bent over it. It was a small notice, not more than a narrow column wide and about three inches long. Each word I read gave me goose bumps, and I felt outside of the whole thing. Like I wasn't the said Rebekah Blount or that this was really a scenario from a movie script.

"That will appear twice more and then we're home free, Becky." Tom's arm was around my shoulders.

I wanted to be their child legally, the same as I was theirs by our mutual love. But supposing my rightful, natural parents read that notice? I mean what if they really showed up? They'd have priority rights, and. . . . I felt sick just thinking about that possibility. And then I got another sick feeling. What if they read it and *didn't* show up?

I must have stiffened or twitched or something because I felt Tom's hand gently press my shoulder.

"Don't worry, Becky. There aren't going to be any hitches." He said it like he was positive, but it sent a chill down my back.

The next notice appeared and we still hadn't

heard from anyone. Tom glowed. "They get one week more, only one measly week more, and then you're OURS!" He looked like a little kid who just had his favorite dessert put in front of him.

"Rosey, I think we can call our lawyer tomorrow and have him get things rolling."

She just shook her head no and said she thought it was a good idea to have something else on our minds until everything was final. "Rebekah, you know we need a solid week to think about that art program you were telling us you're interested in."

I honestly wasn't all that interested in any art program. I had only mentioned to Rosemary that my school was having a poster contest on energy conservation. But I didn't feel like doing anything until my status got settled. I wanted to know if I was going to be Rebekah Lawrence for real, forever.

Actually, the next week didn't drag the way I thought it would. I got caught up in the program in spite of how I felt. There was so much competition for the poster prize that each grade worked as a unit, and I spent most afternoons busy at school.

Then the last notice appeared in the paper, publicly summoning any living soul who cared anything at all for Rebekah Blount. Nobody answered. So nobody cared.

Rosemary and Tom called their lawyer, and they made plans for all of us to go to court, where you go through an actual ceremony. It was like getting married. Only, in a weird way, it felt more like a divorce—a divorce from everything that had been my life up to that point.

That night I went into my room and wrote Mildred a letter. It was filled with a lot of the strange sadness I felt. Like life had cheated us out of something it had no right to and how I wished that somehow we could have a lifelong friendship in spite of the different places we lived and a lot of stuff like that. I also told her I thought about her all the time and hoped she was getting along okay. When I finished I didn't even read it over—you know, how you do for spelling and to see if it sounds the way you meant it to. Instead of doing that, I folded it and tore it into little strips. Then I closed my fingers over the strips, made a fist, walked out to the incinerator in the hallway outside our apartment, and dropped the letter in.

CHAPTER 10

After nobody claimed me, I tried to console myself by telling myself that the Blounts hadn't seen the notice, or, if they had, they had decided not to interfere because they felt this was best for me. Or maybe Blount was really a fake name, and my real parents would never know what had happened to me. Any way I looked at it, though, it was like I was in a state of uncertainty. Something was unfinished.

I was having a hard time straightening out my muddled feelings about my own parents not wanting me and strangers who did. But I loved Rosemary and Tom too much to keep laying my confusion on them. I'd said enough already. The fantastic way they were carrying on, I couldn't spoil it. It was as if their decision to adopt someone had been made the minute they got married and getting me thirteen years later was the answer to their long search.

So I let them see just the happy side of what I felt—that I couldn't believe how my life had changed from Cinderella to the Princess. But even so, I wasn't 100 percent ready to let go of knowing I was really somebody's abandoned kid.

Gradually, I guess, I began to forget how I felt deep inside. Maybe it was the way Rosemary and Tom shared with me. I mean it was, "Rebekah, any ideas on what we should do this weekend?" It was "we" or "us," like a family. And asking my opinion on things like, "How do you feel about junior high school kids experimenting with drugs?" Some difference from what I'd been used to, where no questions ever got asked, only orders given.

And then the girls. They'd say things like, "You've got the coolest parents, Rebekah."

I began to feel as though they really were mine.

Finally, I got knots inside me from hiding the truth from my new friends.

"Rosemary!" I yelled to her one day. "I have to confess."

She looked at me evenly.

"Confess what?" she asked.

She always seems to know when she should—or shouldn't—get upset. It was obvious to her even before I said a word that my confession was not likely to be cause for alarm.

"I have to *tell* everybody that we adopted each other—you and me and Tom."

She grinned slowly. "We've been waiting a long time for that, Sweetheart, haven't we?"

"It's been a while," I smiled back.

"Wanna have a party?"

"Ooh? Super!"

That's how it happened that Rosemary and

Tom gave me a combination birthday and adoption party, and planning it, you'd think we were having a wedding.

"What do you think, girls," Tom was as excited as the father of the bride. "Red, white, and blue decorations?"

"I vote for that," Rosemary said.

The way I felt, it could have been that plus stars and stripes.

"And flowers. What kind do you want, Becky?"

"Gee, I don't know." I wasn't really getting *married*.

Then Rosemary came up with, "Do you want to make your own invitations?"

"Oh boy," I said. "Rosemary, you finally made it."

"Meaning?"

"Meaning, you couldn't do better if you had twelve years practice at motherhood. You know who makes their own invitations?"

"Give me a hint."

"Six-year-olds, that's who."

"So what's that got to do with how I finally arrived at motherhood?"

"All the kids complain that their mothers are out of touch with what's going on in the real world."

"Well, I'm glad I'm on track. I might add, kiddo, ditto for you."

"Meaning?"

"You sound like those daughters mothers refer to as twelve going on thirty."

"Watch out you two." Tom tapped us on our shoulders. "I'm getting jealous and might go find me a son one of these days."

"Don't you dare," I said. "I like it just the way it is."

"I don't know, Becky. You might like it even better with, say, a big, handsome, fifteen-year-old brother."

"Nah," I said. "That's what I want for a boyfriend, not a brother."

We all laughed, and I actually blushed like a dummy, but I wondered a little if Tom really missed not having a boy.

Right then though, the only hurdle I had to get over was telling the girls the real reason I was having a party.

The next morning at breakfast, I was slowly chewing cornflakes and banana circles, thinking about how I was going to break the news. Tom was still shaving, and Rosemary was deciding what she was going to have with her coffee.

"What if I just come right out with it, Rosemary, and tell the kids the facts?"

"Well, natch. How else? Did you taste the pineapple Danish?"

"Does the pineapple Danish have anything to do with my party?"

"Not a thing. I only wanted to know if you tried it and if it's worth eating."

"I did and it's so-so. What shall I say to everybody?"

She fork-stabbed an English muffin and put it in the toaster before she turned to me. "Sweetie, my only suggestion is, don't beat around the bush. Get right to the point."

I had trouble swallowing the mouthful of cereal I'd taken. "Do you think I have to tell them about Meacham?"

There was a penetrating look, and it was a moment before she answered. "That's part of it, isn't it?"

"But that's over."

She gave me a soft look and a smile. "That's what we're happy about. It's over."

I took a deep breath. If I could remember that, it would make it easier for me when I told them.

It wasn't so bad. After all, I didn't have to go into any gruesome details. They weren't really too familiar with Meacham, so that was one good thing. One of the girls even went overboard and said sometimes she was so annoyed with her mother she wished she was adopted and could go find her real parents—who'd have to be an improvement. A couple of the others told her she was being tactless. Outside of that, nobody made any wrong remarks.

But anyway, the party was something. I know I'll remember it all my life. There were the eight of us who were at the sleepover at Karen's, and one more.

"Say, I have an idea I'd like to throw out to you." Tom was always coming up with exciting new ideas.

"What?" I asked, expectantly.

"How about having all your old friends from the dorm? It would be a nice reunion."

That shook me up a little.

"I'd like to throw that idea out too, Tom. Out the window." I guess Rosemary was a little shook by the idea too.

"What do you mean?" He looked at her in surprise.

I wondered if Rosemary was thinking the same thing I was, that the combination might not work. I mean, Hillcrest and Meacham County? Not exactly go-togethers, like bacon and eggs. I loved the kids from Meacham all right, but to be honest I was afraid they'd do or say something to embarrass me. Of course I hated myself for that disloyalty, but it was how I felt.

Rosemary explained to Tom. "I mean I'm not sure it's such a good mix. Not this time, in any case."

She *was* thinking the same way I was.

"They're all her friends, aren't they?" He looked from Rosemary to me, frowning.

"Yes, of course they are, Tom. Maybe next time. . . ." She turned to face me. "What do you think, Rebekah?"

But Tom didn't give me a chance to answer or even to think about an answer. "What's going to be different next time?" he asked, getting a little annoyed.

They weren't going to have another argument on account of me!

"Well, Rebekah might feel she needs more time. To feel more secure about things."

She was defending me, and she shouldn't have to do that. I ought to be speaking up for myself!

But Tom got in ahead of me again. "Look, I don't know what you're worried about. They're all good kids. Have faith in them."

Faith. Rosemary had told me back in September to have faith in my new friends. Maybe Tom was right. Anyway, I wanted to see the argument end.

"That—uh—that might not be such a bad idea —having them now, I mean."

Rosemary looked at me, surprised. "Well, okay. If that's what you *really* want, Rebekah."

I gulped down to my toes. I wasn't at all sure it was what I wanted. But at least there wasn't going to be any more fighting. Tom was already working on the details.

"I could borrow the Johnson's station wagon and fit the whole mob in comfortably."

Too late to back out now. Maybe I *was* a rotten person for not being sure. I wasn't even sure why the idea had bothered me so. But I wasn't going to think about it. It was settled, and, for good or bad, Meacham was coming to Hillcrest.

I sent out one invitation for all the Meacham girls. Mildred wrote back. "Thanks for asking us. We'll come! Love. Your pals."

About a week before the party, Miss Crane called and explained to Rosemary that Kathy's psychiatrist didn't want her to attend. Even though I was relieved, I was ashamed for feeling it. Then the morning of the party Tom answered a phone call from Baker, who told him that Allie, Marie, Madelaine, and Mary Ellen had just come down with the flu.

I felt as if I'd made it happen by my rotten thoughts.

"She's lying," I said. "How come she's letting Mildred out?"

"She specifically told me that Mildred had it last week."

"I bet she's sorry Mildred's better," I said hotly. I meant it, too.

Tom didn't even make me take back what I said.

So he picked up Mildred, alone, in our car, and by the time they got back, everyone else had arrived.

While I still had doubts about my old friends mixing with my new ones, I'd never thought specifically about what could happen. But when Mildred came in the door, it was like she was Exhibit A. Who would have known she'd be wearing a coat that looked like something my Hillcrest friends would have given to Goodwill? Even though Terry, Karen, and the others didn't stare or make her feel tacky, I wondered what they were really thinking.

"Let's hang your coat right here in the guest closet." Tom started helping her off with it, and I saw that the dress she had on was just as shabby as the coat. I felt for just a moment like we were strangers. It *had* been a long time. Then she handed me something, smiling shyly. I looked down at a flat package, about six inches square. It was wrapped in Happy Birthday paper, but because the package was so small the writing on it only got as far as Happy Birthd. My heart took a dive. The girls will laugh at something wrapped like that. Or they'll make cracks—to themselves, if not to me.

I became aware of the presence of the girls behind me and felt rotten about myself. It was the beginning of a long day of swerving from one extreme to the other, thinking first of Meacham and then of Hillcrest.

"Thanks, Mildred," I said, taking the present. "Oh—uh—come on in and meet everyone."

I started introducing, and Karen took the package out of my hands. I felt my heart stopping. What was she doing with it?

"That goes in the box with the rest of your gifts," she said, and walked away with it.

"Mildred, I feel as if I've known you as long as

I've known Rebekah." Rosemary was in the middle of the group reaching out both her arms to Mildred. "Rebekah talks about you so often."

I shot Rosemary a glance. She wasn't being sarcastic, I knew that, but I felt sleazy considering the kind of "talk" I'd had with Rosemary about Mildred and the others.

Then the party got rolling, with Tom making his fabulous chicken barbecue. He did it on the grill on our balcony. In anything short of a blizzard, Tom is out there wearing his denim jacket, freezing his hands off and making mouth-watering creations. Actually, watching him was half the fun that day.

"Wait till I tell *my* father what *your* father can do," Terry grinned, making a very big hit with Tom.

Then when we got to the dining room, Karen said excitedly, "Ooh, what gorgeous place markers! They match the invitations!"

And another girl said, "I saw them in Scott's Stationery Store, Rebekah. They're fabulous!"

Rosemary and I exchanged significant looks. That was one of the times during the day when I felt very Number Ten Oakdale Circle.

So far as anyone else could tell, it was a wonderful party. I mean, if you only listened to the general babble of our voices and saw us bouncing around, it *looked* like a wonderful party. But it wasn't the way it would have been if only the kids from the neighborhood were there. I mean, there it was. Mildred looked like she knew she didn't belong.

All at once I felt as if I were back in the District 12 School defending her against Kevin Schultz.

"Hey, Mildred, you're sitting next to me," I called out to her. "You're my guest of honor." She looked kind of bewildered and didn't move, so I went over and sort of led her to where her place was.

"Gee, Rebekah," she whispered, "this sure isn't like the birthdays at Meacham."

"You're darn right." I enthusiastically squeezed her arm and then, realizing the effect of what I said, I felt horrible. I didn't seem to be getting anything right.

I wanted to say more. I wanted to say something like, "Hey Mildred, maybe your mother will get you out of there by *your* next birthday." She was going to be thirteen in April, but I didn't have any reason to believe that miracle would happen by then. So I had to remind myself to shut up, and that made it kind of hard to have a satisfactory conversation with her.

We all gorged ourselves on the food, and then Terry carried in the cake. I didn't know in advance what the decoration or the writing on it was going to be since all the girls insisted on pitching in for it as a surprise. Terry put it in front of me with all the candles lit. The whole top was covered with the words: Happy Birthday to the New Family—Rebekah and her Mother and Father. The rest of the frosting had hearts all over it. First I squealed and then I cried. Everybody's face blurred into everybody else's. Mildred's might have been different, but I didn't dare look. How could she be enjoying herself when all this was for me and she had nothing?

"Make a wish! Make a wish!"

It seemed to me as if everyone thought that whatever I wished would come true. If I hadn't had that sinking feeling about Mildred, I would have been sure there was nothing left to wish for. I had everything.

Everybody sang Happy Birthday, Happy Adoption, Happy New Family, and I still couldn't look in Mildred's direction. After the cake and ice cream, Karen went into the living room and came back with a cardboard carton covered with silver foil and ribbon. That was the box that was filled with presents, and I just stared at it, speechless.

"Open them. Open them, Rebekah!"

I reached in the carton, fumbled with the wrappings, and opened one spectacular gift after another. Each one was the kind that we kids at Meacham never imagined. I got earrings, records, a scarf and glove set that was very different but reminded me of the recycled mittens.

I took out another package wrapped in plain pink paper with yellow ribbon. Strong's Jeweler's it said on the cover of the white box. Another pair of earrings, I thought. I'm dreaming. The star-shaped ones from Karen were for pierced ears, and Rosemary had said when I couldn't try them on, "Monday, I'm leaving the office early. We have a date to get your ears pierced." I was floating.

The room was quiet as I undid the yellow bow and lifted off the cover. I removed the cotton pad that showed a purple velvet jewel case, and I gasped. The purple velvet top opened with a small snap. Feeling like a queen on a throne, I saw a heart-shaped locket and a chain of pure gold. There was no question that it was gold. I think my hand was sweating when I touched it. I couldn't even swallow as I opened the heart. In tiny but very clear printing it read: To our dearest daughter, Rebekah. And then it had the date. On either side was a smiling snapshot of Rosemary and Tom.

"What does it SAY?" someone prodded.

I couldn't see through the blur, but I didn't need to read the words. "To our dearest. . . ." that was as far as I could get, and Rosemary and Tom were standing beside me. I stood up too, and I remember getting pretty well wrapped up in their arms. The three of us could have been alone somewhere in the Sahara Desert for all it mattered about anyone else. Then Tom stood behind me with the locket and put it around my neck.

The girls crowded around me to look and to touch.

"Gorgeous!"

"Heavenly!"

I was on a cloud. Maybe there are other ways to describe my feeling—I don't know them.

"Hey, here's another present," someone picked up the last one in the box.

"Who's it from?"

"From the guest of honor," Rosemary said, and we all looked at Mildred.

"Quick, open it," Terry urged, handing it to me.

I threw Rosemary a tragic glance. She smiled at me encouragingly. I looked back at the package and tore off the Scotch tape. My hand was trembling, I'm pretty sure. What could she have bought? After all, money isn't something any Meacham resident gets to handle.

I opened the box and made myself look. A color snapshot showed Mildred and the rest of my dorm mates standing in front of Building A, all smiling at me as if they were the happiest kids in the world. My heart skipped a few beats. So what if Mildred was wearing old clothes? So what if nobody in the snapshot looked like a Gucci ad? Was that all that mattered? I took the picture out, and under it, on construction paper, was a handmade greeting: "Happy Birthday, Rebekah *Lawrence* from your old buddies," it said, and they had all signed their names.

"Do you like it?" I raised my head at Mildred's quiet question.

"Ohh . . . Mildred. It's beautiful," I said, and I felt unworthy. "Honest, it's beautiful!"

"Miss Crane took it with her camera. It was the day before I came down with the flu. The rest of the kids felt terrible they couldn't make it today."

I wished I had postponed the party until they all could have come—Goodwill clothes and all.

"I do, too," I said. I hoped she believed me.

At the end of the party, when everyone went home and Tom drove Mildred back, I thought about the letter I had written her before. I wished I could get it back from the incinerator so I could paste all the pieces back together again. This time I'd send it for sure.

CHAPTER 11

It was February. Seven months since I'd become Rebekah Lawrence, one month since the party and since I'd written a thank-you note to all the Meacham kids. I told them I had their picture on my desk and still felt very close to them.

That was true all right, but looking at them made me sad. Definitely the opposite feeling from the one you're supposed to have when you look at the grinning faces of your friends. I didn't know for sure if it was because I missed them or what. We'd had a lot of stormy weather in January, so it hadn't been practical to have them over.

I suppose it's easy to find excuses. Rosemary says that people don't have any trouble doing the things they want to do. So that means if I didn't have them over, I didn't want to. Why didn't I? I knew all right. Down deep I knew. No matter what I had said to myself the day of my party, I still couldn't get myself to accept that what they looked or acted like wasn't important. And in spite of how well the party went, I was worried about what Terry and the others thought. If they thought Mildred was weird, then that had to be the way they felt about me.

It was a Friday night and Rosemary, Tom, and I were in the den just sitting around deciding if we'd read, look at TV, or talk. It turned out we talked. Well, actually, it started out like one of those close-knit family heart-to-heart talks and ended up with almost mouth-to-mouth yelling. If I was going to describe it like a play, I'd begin by saying: Tom, sitting relaxed in a leather chair, stage left, speaks:

"Becky, we've been thinking, Rosey and I, about enlarging the family—but we want to know how you feel about it, of course."

I know I must have turned red. Of course I know all about how people have babies—Rosemary had straightened me out on any fuzzy ideas I might have had on the subject—but thinking about it in relation to Tom and Rosemary made me so embarrassed I could hardly look at either one of them. Besides, if they wanted to have a baby, why did they think they had to get my approval?

"Oh," I said, hoping what was in my mind didn't show on my face, and then I couldn't say anything more because I didn't know what to say.

I heard Rosemary's voice. "Sweetie, you know how much Tom has wanted a son."

My face must have shown something I wasn't aware of for her to make that appeal. After all, I hadn't said anything against their proposition.

Then I thought, how can you work it so you get the right sex kid you want? Science must have progressed a lot lately.

"Last summer, when we talked with Miss Crane," Tom was saying, "they didn't have a boy the right age for us, and since we've had you, we've been so happy we haven't thought of anyone else."

Oh. They meant adopt someone, like they did with me. Not have a baby. That was different!

"You've made us a family, Becky, and it's been so good, we've been thinking, maybe more is better. How does that strike you?"

I didn't know—it was so sudden.

"How do you feel about it, honey? Are you ready for a brother?"

A brother? Say, this was no play. Tom really did want a boy, and they were serious about finding one to adopt. This was for real.

Was I ready, Rosemary wanted to know. Well, no. No, I wasn't. I thought all they wanted was me. That happiness Tom said they had was on account of *me*. How could they think of anyone else! A *stranger*. The more I thought about it, the angrier I got. I felt an ache in my head, and I wanted to let them know exactly how I felt. I looked at Rosemary. Somehow she was the one I wanted to lash out at.

"How *could* you?" I spit the words at her.

She couldn't have looked more hurt than if I'd slapped her. She jumped up from the sofa and held her arms wide apart, like I was supposed to let her hug me. But I wasn't having any part of that.

"Rebekah, dear." She caressed my cheek with one hand and smoothed my hair with the other. "I understand why you're upset. Listen, nothing is going to change right away. We'll talk about it some more later, okay?"

I was breathing hard. The thing was, I didn't think I was wrong to feel so angry. Maybe more is better? That's what Tom said. Wasn't I enough?

"Are you going to have a house like Meacham? Am I going to have to live in a dorm instead of a bedroom?" I was really fuming.

"Hey, wait a minute, Becky girl." Tom's voice carried a lot of authority, and it made me look at him.

"We're not interested in grabbing every kid who needs a home. We're not that good-hearted." He wasn't looking good-hearted when he said it either. "We're just ordinary people, and all we want is a conventional happy family."

"Don't I make a conventional happy family? Plenty of people only have one child. I don't want a brother."

Rosemary looked in pain. Then she said, in a pleading tone, "It's just somebody more we can all love, honey."

I didn't pay any attention to what she was trying to get across. "I don't need anyone else to love."

"You sure do, Rebekah Lawrence. Everybody does."

Tom didn't call me Becky. He probably hates me, I thought, and he'll want to get rid of me. Well let him! I stood up with a jerk and ran out of the room, yelling, "I knew it wouldn't last. Nothing good in my life ever lasted!"

"*What* hasn't lasted?" Tom's voice was stern and growing louder as I reached the door of my bedroom.

"Rebekah, you don't mean that!" Rosemary was close to shouting.

I slammed my door and just stood there. I was totally ashamed at how unhinged I'd acted, but I still didn't want anybody else moving in with us. Darn, darn! I wished the conversation had never happened. I wished Tom and Rosemary felt I was the only child in the world they could ever love. Why couldn't it be like that?

For a long time no sound came from any of the other rooms. Did they go out? Did they abandon me, too, like the others did? Well, I probably wasn't worth anything better. What good was I anyway? I might as well. . . .

"Okay, Becky, you can come out now."

"C'mon, honey."

"Hey, we're not going to talk about it any more today."

"Let's have some of those toll house cookies, the ones left from what we made last week."

I couldn't face them. I didn't want any cookies.

"Hey, open up—this is the law!" There was a banging on my door.

I reached over and turned the knob. Both of them were standing on the other side. Rosemary took a step forward, and Tom said, "Nothing like a good fight to prove we're a real family, right, Beck?"

I tried to make a convincing smile.

What were they going to do now, I wondered. Not adopt someone because I couldn't handle it, or go ahead with their plans no matter how I felt? Either way it wasn't right, because someone was going to be miserable. By rights, it should be me, I thought. I'd have to pretend I could see what a great idea it really was when I stopped and thought about it.

"Did you have someone special in mind?" I asked. "I mean, have you found a—a boy yet?"

"Look, the discussion is closed for the present— okay?" Tom looked straight at me and waited, as if for a sign that it *was* okay with me.

How could I let them leave it that way? I opened my mouth for some lie to come out, but Rosemary stopped me.

"Don't worry about it, honey. Don't even think about if for now, you hear? We're not."

That's what they said, and I wanted to believe them. So I tried to put it out of my mind.

CHAPTER 12

Two weeks passed, and nobody said anything more. About the subject of another adoption, I mean. Only, the next day Rosemary made an effort to reassure me again. Tom was working with some clients, and the opera was on the radio. Rosemary had been trying, without any luck, to get me to appreciate that screeching, and after what seemed to her a particularly moving scene, she said, "Sweetheart, you're not brooding about last night, are you?"

I wished she'd quit it. I figured if she was going to keep on bringing it up it would never get settled. I shook my head no.

Then the soprano let out a big yelp, and Rosemary's attention fortunately got diverted from me.

But at supper that night it seemed to me that Tom was bending over backwards to be cheerful and funny. Not that he wasn't always good-natured and all, but I had this feeling he was forcing it. Still, like I said, the subject didn't come up again for two weeks.

It was in March that things started happening. One day I came home from school and picked up the mail, like I usually do. That day there was a letter for me, a fat one. It was from Mildred. I waited until I got to my room and sat down at my desk to open it. It's a wonder I didn't close my door, even though nobody else was home. Sometimes you do funny things.

The letter went like this: "Dear Rebekah; a lot has happened since I saw you. I think outside of the things I'm going to tell you that happened, everything is the same here. You-know-who is still in charge; the food and the rules are the same too. What is different is that Miss Crane has been smiling a lot lately. We haven't figured out if it's because she's in love or if she's getting fired. The other changes are in our dorm. Madelaine and Allie have been in foster homes for a few weeks. Madelaine got in with a family that has eleven other foster kids that they've had for practically all their lives—the kids' lives, I mean. So Madelaine thinks this might be for keeps for her too. She's glad, of course. Allie's not sure about her family. After she was there for a week, she came back, and now they're trying it again. She said she doesn't know if they'll get along.

"The worst thing is about Kathy. She had to leave. They said she wasn't making progress, and she's at McLean. You know, that hospital where all those special doctors are. I keep thinking how awful she must feel without her friends to cheer her up. I mean, I think if your friends can't be there when you need them, what good are friends?

"We also have a new girl, Doreen. She scares me the way she looks at you know who. Marie says you-know-who has met her match. I don't know.

"That's about all from here. How are you? Your party was great. I told everyone all about it. They were sorry to miss it. They all send love. Regards to your mother and father. This took a long time to write. Mildred.
P.S. My mother came last week. She said, maybe next year. M."

I felt ten times sadder reading that letter than when I looked at the smiling snapshot picture. I mean, it was pretty clear from Mildred how intimidated she was by Baker—she couldn't even write down her name. All that you-know-who stuff. Also, she probably figured that if Doreen was going to stand up to Baker, Mildred would be at the wrong end of the trouble, as always. And that bit about her mother. Maybe next year. Why did she have to tell her that? It had to be a lie. And knowing Mildred, she didn't tell anyone about how I didn't pay attention to her at the party. She probably said a bunch of good things I didn't deserve. But that stuff she said about Kathy with no friends to cheer her up —she had to be referring to me. Mildred could use me now, and I was letting her down again.

I wanted to write to her that minute. This time my letter wouldn't be filled with gloom. This time it would be more like, "Dear Mildred; I know that Kathy is going to be all right. So will Allie. Isn't it terrific about Madelaine? Good for Doreen! Maybe she'll get Baker fired. Just think, in one year you'll be out of there, back at home with your wonderful mother. Love and keep smiling. Rebekah."

But even Mildred would see through that baloney. And she might figure, sure it's easy for Rebekah to be cheerful. She's in a comfortable, happy home with loving parents, delicious food, and good clothes.

Mildred would be right too. It would be easy for me to write like that and easy for me to be a big shot and forget how intimidated I had been by you-know-who.

Suddenly I crumpled up her letter and threw it in my waste basket. Then I felt ashamed and took it back and smoothed it out. But I shoved it under some things in my desk drawer and didn't even try to write an answer.

I looked at the clock on my night-table. Four-thirty. Rosemary and Tom usually came in around half-past five. That gave me an hour. Plenty of time to go into the kitchen and check out what was on the list for me to do for dinner.

Our kitchen is one of those last-word affairs with the latest appliances. Anytime I see commercials on TV advertising dishwashing liquid, I wonder who's buying that stuff. I mean, since I've gotten out into the real world I haven't met anyone who doesn't own an automatic dishwasher. It's funny how easily you can go from a deprived environment to a we-have-everything one and forget. That's one of the things that bothers me.

I looked on the corkboard beside the refrigerator. Under Thursday it read:

Chili and corn bread
green salad
blueberry pudding

We have a well-organized arrangement. We Lawrences, I mean. Saturday mornings are reserved for planning the week's menu, shopping for the food, and making a schedule for who does what. And when. On this corkboard we list the chores for the week as well as recipes for certain foods. So whoever gets home first will maybe set the table, wash and prepare the vegetables, turn on the oven if necessary, and everything like that. Whoever comes in after that takes over wherever the Number 1 person is at. It's a nice way to run things. I mean, that way it's like a team.

"Hi," the Number 2 person coming in calls out, "anybody home?"

"Number 1 person in kitchen," is the usual answer. Usually me.

When Number 3 person comes in, it's a breeze to put the finish on the whole meal. Then we all sit down to eat and start talking back and forth about our day. If anyone has a big problem, that's the one who starts talking first. The others listen, make suggestions or just sympathize, and then someone else gets a turn. Our mealtimes are used to deal with the things that matter to each of us, and that makes them important to us all. During those times it's easy to forget my past.

I had all the ingredients for the chili out and was stirring the corn bread batter when I heard the front door open and Tom's voice.

"I think Becky will understand when we tell her the whole story."

Tell me what?

"I hope so. We'll find out soon enough. Hello, anybody home?"

"Number 1 person in the kitchen," I answered.

"Becky, we have something important to tell you." They both came into the kitchen, and I could see Tom was excited. "You know Charlie Taylor, Becky?"

I did. He had the desk next to Tom's in their real estate office.

"Well, his neighbors, the Saxons, had friends in Vermont, and last year, when they were in France, they had a terrible accident. They were mountain climbing and—"

"Tom," Rosemary interrupted, "Rebekah doesn't need the gory details."

I was wondering what all this was leading up to.

"You're right, Rosey. I'll get to the point." Tom gave me his full attention. "When we talked about adopting a boy, we said we wouldn't bring it up again soon. We'd give you some time to think about it, get used to the idea."

I felt a terrible thud in my chest. I had told myself I would pretend for their sake. They must have thought I was ready, but I wasn't.

"Now something has come up, and we *have* to discuss it with you."

Rosemary said gently and earnestly, "Sweetie, this is a pretty big piece of news. We've known about that accident, but we didn't know until today that there was a boy your age involved." The look in her eyes told me she wanted him—the boy. I didn't care how old he was. I didn't want him.

"His parents were killed in that mountain climb. His name is David, and he's been living in Denver with his uncle, a bachelor, who travels a lot for his job and—"

"And," Tom cut in, "the uncle decided he has to give the boy up, and that's where we come in."

They were finished with their news, and my head was spinning. I tried to say something, but no words came out.

Then Tom said, very soberly, "It would be a blessing if we could give Davy a new start, to try to make up to him for his loss."

"But we want you to feel right about this."

"We know how you felt when we talked about it before, and we didn't want to just spring it on you. But under the circumstances waiting would be a mistake."

Tom wanted a boy so much he was already using a nickname for him. How could I do anything but agree?

So I tried. I tried with every bit of spunk I felt I was made of. And I knew I had to look right at them while I talked so they could see that I meant it. I deliberately lifted my chin and put on one of those real positive expressions, like I admired them for their wonderful unselfishness and I couldn't agree more.

"That's really super," I lied. "I mean, the poor kid—do you think you'll really be able to adopt him?"

"It looks pretty certain."

I thought Rosemary didn't believe my enthusiasm 100 percent, and she asked me, "Are you sure you wouldn't be unhappy if we did this?"

"I'm *sure*."

Rosemary fell for it and practically flung her arms around me. Tom didn't say anything, but he looked at me with such pride that I almost wished that what I had said was the truth. For the rest of the dinner preparation, I kept my self-control. Tom got the silverware out of the drawer and just stood there and grinned, looking as if he'd forgotten what he was supposed to do with it.

"That's for setting the table, Tommy." Rosemary gave him a kiss on the cheek.

She didn't often call him Tommy. There was no question about the excitement they felt over the prospect of getting that boy. She took the dishes off the shelf, and they both went into the dining room. I kept saying over and over to myself that they wanted a bigger family because having me had made them so happy. But maybe that wasn't it at all. Maybe the truth was that they hoped they'd do better with another kid.

My head was really hurting. This was a lot to take for one day. Actually more like one hour, since I had also gotten Mildred's letter, full of her troubles. Allie and Madelaine were gone, that new girl was sure to get Mildred in bad with Baker, and her mother would never take her. She needed me now more than she ever did, and if I had any character left at all I'd go back.

Go back? What was I telling myself? I felt a throbbing in my temples, and I started to shake. I had to grab onto the long neck of the kitchen faucet to steady myself. Crazy. I was going crazy, like they thought Kathy was. I had the best set-up any kid in the world could want—the impossible dream of my whole life had come true . . . until now. . . .

"Is the chili ready for serving, Rebekah?" Rosemary called from the dining room.

I let go of the faucet and knew I had to calm down—fast.

"I'll check it," I answered.

It was ready. We put everything on the table and sat down to eat.

Since I was the one with the problem that night, I should have started the dinner conversation. But I didn't. Even if I had been in the mood, I wouldn't have gotten the chance. Practically the only time Tom took out from talking about my "brother" was when he pierced the corn bread with his fork to cool it off and watched the four little breathing holes give off steam. Rosemary didn't say much, but I could tell she approved of everything Tom was saying.

So far as I was concerned, the food tasted like Christy's. I felt a hundred years old by the end of the meal and almost as if you-know-who had been standing there intimidating me.

CHAPTER 13

That night the telephone calls started. First it was from the uncle in Denver, then from Vermont, then the Saxons, then back to Denver.

Why don't the Saxons take him, I suddenly thought. They were the ones who were friends of his parents! I couldn't stand the way Tom was acting and knowing that when this kid got on the scene, Rosemary would be up on a cloud somewhere, like she used to be with me. I was being replaced.

I don't think they even heard me when I said I was going into my room to do homework. I managed to keep my mind on the assignment in spite of being reminded again of Mildred when I reached into my desk drawer for a pen and accidentally touched her wrinkled letter.

I was going to her. And this time I wasn't kidding. I meant it. I had to figure out a plan—how and when—but I was going. I was sure now. More than when I first thought of it. Those telephone calls sounded like final arrangements were being worked out. My lips curved down and quivered. That new boy was putting me in the background. I was glad my homework wasn't too complicated. I finished it and went to bed.

One good thing happened the next day. Our report cards came out. I got four Bs and one A—in science. I got warm all over when I looked at my grades. That A really lifted me way off the ground. I decided then and there that I was going to major in science for my life's work. During the whole bus ride home from school I kept feeling in my pocket for the envelope the report was in. I didn't even take my hand out of that pocket—just kept fingering the rectangular outline and patting the flat side. Can you picture that? Patting it! You'd think I was Mildred with one of those letters from her mother.

My decision about science had nothing to do with my plan to leave, though.

Terry and Karen got good marks too, so we decided to blow what was left of our week's allowance on double-dip sundaes at Sunshine's, our favorite ice-cream place. A celebration.

Sunshine's is our favorite place because Karen has this mad crush on Tippy Farnum who works behind the counter. Tippy is eighteen years old and is graduating from high school in June. Personally, I think she's out of her mind wasting a perfectly good crush on a boy that old. And going away to college next year, too.

"Let's go to Sunshine's before we go home," Karen had said when school was over. "I'm starving."

"Starving for what?" Terry teased her.

"Vanilla," I said, which was kind of an inside joke with us. Nobody orders vanilla. I mean, it's so nothing. But Karen gets so flustered when Tippy waits on her that all she can say is that she wants a jumbo-sized vanilla cone. And then she eats it without even realizing what she's doing. If you ask me, she should try and control her feelings. It doesn't always work, though, as I know very well.

After Karen tried to hide a big smile over what we knew she was really starving for, I said, "Let's go home first. I don't want anything to happen to my report card in the mob scene at Sunshine's."

"Right," Terry said. "You might never get another one like it. Better put it in the safe."

"I'll do just that," I said.

While we were kidding around my problems just weren't in the picture. I wonder if that's the way it is with most people. I mean, there I was going through the day enjoying the good parts and forgetting the bad. Times like those, too, I never had any misgivings about how my friends felt about me.

We decided to meet at the corner as soon as we all put our report cards under guard.

I unlocked the front door and heard Rosemary's voice. "I agree," she was saying.

She never comes home from work just like that in the middle of the day. I mean she didn't sound sick. I walked over and stood beside her at the phone.

"Yes, that will be fine, Mr. Fernald. You know our address . . . yes . . . whenever it's comfortable for you. About 5:00? Fine. Thank *you*. Goodbye."

She hung up and looked at me. I could tell right away. She had a gleam in her eyes. That meant the call was either to Denver, Vermont, or the Saxons. I just stood there, waiting. Waiting for her to tell me what she really didn't have to. That kid was on his way. To our house.

"Rebekah!" She smiled wide, and her cheeks filled out like rosy apples. She looked at me with her special happy look. Only this time it wasn't for me. It was for someone else.

"Tomorrow, the Fernalds are bringing David here. Oh, Rebekah, honey," she got up and grabbed me around my waist. Then she stood apart from me, her hands on my shoulders. "How wonderful for us all."

She said it quietly. I mean, she wasn't jumping up and down and like that. But the quiet way she said it made it seem even more meaningful. I thought she expected me to say something, but it was very hard.

"That's great. Really great."

Apparently it didn't make a bit of difference. I could just as well have said, "Rats. Who wants him?" and she wouldn't have heard me. I wondered if she'd lost that insight she used to have. Knowing what I was feeling or thinking whether I said it out loud or not.

"Now listen, honey." It was like she quickly came back to earth. "He'll sleep in the den, of course. It's lucky we have that sleep-couch in there. Oh I hope he *stays!* We'll have to get a bigger place—a house. Yes, a *house.* Oh this is absolutely sublime!"

Absolutely sick, is what. She must have taken the afternoon off from work just so she could get on the telephone and make arrangements for him to come. And now she's ready to move out of here. This is the first honest-to-goodness house I ever knew that I felt was home. But it doesn't mean anything to her. All she wants is a big house so that . . . *he* will be comfortable. I'm not important to her anymore. The same thing is happening all over again—I was right. I love someone and it ends.

I bit my lip and then pressed my teeth down hard. I was not going to give in to trembling and crying. I put my hand in my pocket for my handkerchief and felt an envelope. My report card. In my mind, I saw what might have taken place if this situation had never come up.

"Rosemary," I would have said casually, "I got my report card today."

"Let's *see* it." She would have been full of eagerness.

"Oh, its nothing special," I would have pretended, enjoying the suspense.

Then when Tom came home we'd go through some of the same business, and finally, when they looked at it, all their buttons would pop with pride, and we'd all start talking about how I was going to win the Nobel Prize in physics. I'd be another Marie Curie and my discoveries would make the name Rebekah Lawrence live forever.

Sure.

"Uh—I told the girls I'd meet them. We're going to Sunshine's. We—I won't be long. Okay?"

"All right, sweetheart. Have fun. I've got to call Tom." She gave me a peck on the cheek, not noticing that I hadn't gotten excited.

I didn't mention anything about it to Terry or Karen. That would have to wait until I could handle it better. When we got to Sunshine's, I thought I'd order vanilla. A triple decker. It wouldn't matter how it tasted.

The next morning, which was Saturday, Rosemary and Tom were nervously inspecting every room in the apartment, to make sure everything looked the way they wanted it to—clean, neat, all the putaway-ables out of sight, and whatever they wanted him to see in plain view. The Queen of England couldn't have been given a better reception.

"Tom, did you get enough Coke? You know how boys love Coke."

That was too much. Boys love Coke. Girls, particularly those named Rebekah, love vinegar and vanilla ice cream, and most of all they love to be ignored and forgotten like last year's adopted child.

Tom checked the Coke supply. He'd gotten enough the night before for a hundred kids for a year.

Then, as per our regular schedule, we were going over menus for the week and making a shopping list.

"Shall we have a barbecue tonight?"

"Definitely."

"And Sunday dinner. What do you think would be good for Sunday dinner?"

"Ham. Ham is good. Or roast beef. What's your preference, Becky?"

Someone finally got around to noticing that I was alive.

"Either one is fine with me," I said.

"And Rosie, make a chocolate cake. We haven't had one of those for weeks."

I remembered the first one of hers that I ate. The way things were developing, I didn't want to remember.

The phone rang and I froze. Rosemary and Tom both dashed to answer, simultaneously. I didn't know how much more of this I could stand.

"Becky, it's for you—Terry."

"Oh."

I picked up the phone. "Hi."

Terry wanted to know would I go to the movies this afternoon. I'd have said yes to anything the way I felt—even a Mickey Mouse cartoon.

"Sure."

We agreed we'd meet at her house at one o'clock. When I got through with the call, I said, "Terry, Karen, and I are going to the movies this afternoon. Okay?"

"Sure, honey, if that's what you want to do."

I nodded and waited for them to ask me what movie. They always did, just so they'd know. I mean, it wasn't that I ever requested going to an R or an X one, but this time they didn't even care to check.

We went grocery shopping, and I restrained myself from taking a box of sugar-coated cereal off the shelves. We don't have that in the house, but I thought it would be very good for a boy's teeth. He could get a lot of cavities that way.

I managed to get through lunch but kept looking at my watch. Rosemary and Tom were still discussing preparations for the coming event. I knew it would be harder for me to explain why I wasn't excited than it would be for me to pretend sincere interest, so I pretended sincere interest.

"Do you know if this boy—David—is in the seventh grade? That would be wild!"

"Wild meaning good or bad?" I was sure Tom knew what I meant. He just wanted to hear me say it.

"Good," I said, and moved my lips into a big smile.

I could tell from Rosemary's face that really pleased her.

"No one's mentioned what grade he's in," Tom said, "but knowing you, I'm sure you'll help him out wherever he winds up."

I thought I might give up physics for a career and go on the stage. I mean I was really convincing. But at a quarter to one, I felt as if I'd been let out of captivity.

"He'll be here around five o'clock, sweetie.

You'll be home before then, won't you?" She didn't even have to mention his name—I was supposed to understand.

"As soon as the movie lets out—I'll—I'll fly home." My pretending was almost perfect.

"Have fun."

I left and walked three blocks on the mossy sidewalks, which were now covered with globs of crusted snow left over from a recent storm. The city plows the streets, but since they probably don't recognize those mounds as sidewalks, they ignore them. That last storm hadn't been too bad, so walking was no hardship.

Terry's house is five blocks from our building, and by the time I was at the fourth streetcorner waiting for traffic to pass, I knew that I was not going to the movies that day. I didn't have a plan, but I was going to Mildred. I had no luggage, permission from no one, and I knew that Miss Crane might not even be there on Saturday to act as a buffer against any interference from Baker. I didn't care. Mildred needed me, and with that boy coming it was the only and best thing for me to do. And now was the time.

I had to think up an excuse to tell Terry. Something that wouldn't make her suspicious. I slowed my pace for the next block while I figured it out. It couldn't be that I had a toothache or anything like that—after all, I didn't want her calling the house later. Besides I wouldn't want to spoil Rosemary and Tom's day. Let them have their happiness with—with him.

"Terry, I'm a nerd," I said looking straight-faced at her when she opened the door.

"Whadja do wrong?" she asked.

"Actually, I'm probably not supposed to tell you, but—" I lowered my voice and looked around her hallway as if I didn't want anyone else to hear.

"Nobody's home, Rebekah. What's up?" She seemed scared about what my problem might be.

"Well, don't say a word to anyone—except Karen of course—but my parents are going to adopt a boy and he's coming this afternoon and—"

"Rebekah! That's great! Why didn't you tell me?"

I was a little surprised at her reaction, but I went on. "Well, it's not really settled yet. He's well, it's like on trial—you know. Anyway, Rosemary and Tom are busy and excited and I thought it was selfish of me to walk out on them. I really think I ought to go home and—uh—wait with them."

"Natch. Ooh tell me about him. How old is he? Where's he from? Rebekah, that's fabulous!"

I wasn't real sure if she was putting that on. I couldn't actually see what made it so fabulous.

"I—I don't know too much about it. Listen, I've really got to get back. Now I'll call *you* tonight, later, you know, after everything settles down and all. . . ."

"Of course. Oh, wait'll I tell Karen. Call me as soon as you can, Rebekah."

"Right. Sure will. Uh—enjoy the movie. Bye."

I ran across the street toward Oakville Circle,

even though the bus I was going to take was in the opposite direction. I zigged and zagged back to the right street, nervous that I might bump into Karen on her way to Terry's house. When the bus came, I put in the exact change, found out where to get off, and then got a transfer. I sat way in the back, in case somebody I knew got on. I didn't want to have to make up any new explanations.

There weren't too many passengers. That meant not a lot of conversation. I could just look out the window and concentrate. But it didn't work. My brain was a jumble, and my heart was thumping so loudly I half expected the driver to yell out, "No drum beating allowed on this bus!"

"Change for South Huntington," was what he announced instead.

"Wh—Where do I get the bus for. . . ." I felt that if I said Meacham out loud, someone was going to arrest me for being a runaway. Fortunately, the bus driver remembered from when I had whispered it the first time.

"Right there, on that corner, Missy. Have a nice day."

I gulped and tried to say "thank you" but couldn't.

I found myself standing at a busy intersection. There was a bar on the bus stop corner. Lots of people were going inside, and no one was waiting for the bus. The driver was wrong, I was sure. And there I was outside a bar, a long way from anyplace, and it would start to snow and I would get pneumonia and never make it to Mildred.

I heard the squishy sound of a diesel motor and relaxed. The driver had been right. I got on the bus and handed over my transfer. This time I took a seat right near the door. Five stops later, I got off. I was right in front of Meacham.

The tall iron fence and faded red-brick building beyond looked just as grim and unfriendly as I remembered. I had viewed this place a hundred million times. But it still held the same threatening power over me as always. *Ohmygod,* I thought, *how could I have left Mildred in this place? And how can I go back in?*

CHAPTER 14

What happened to my courage? Why didn't I move? Where were my GUTS? It didn't take any guts to decide I was coming back. That was easy, all in the mind. Even getting here was no big deal. I just sat in a bus and somebody drove me. But walking in there, taking one step or raising one hand to open the gate—that took guts, and I just stood there, like my feet were buried in cement.

I looked at my watch. Two o'clock. Lunch would be over, and there wouldn't be any outdoor activity this time of year. The kids could be in any number of different places right now. I swallowed hard. Then I closed my eyes and honest, I heard a voice. Rosemary's. It was like she was standing beside me.

"When you do something for someone else's benefit, it's not like falling off a log—it's not always easy. But you do it because you want to."

I remembered she said that to me when we had been talking about how nice Mr. Johnson, our neighbor, was to loan Tom his station wagon when we thought he'd need it to pick up the Meacham girls for my party. It turned out, of course, that we didn't need it. But we found out later that Mr. Johnson had planned on going way out in the country that day to load his car with logs for his fireplace, and he was ready to change his plans for us. And then Rosemary had said, "You don't do these things to satisfy yourself. It's for the other person."

Remembering that, I pushed Meacham's iron gate open and walked toward the front door like I was in a hypnotic state. No, that's not right. I knew exactly what I was doing, but it was as if I was getting guidance. From Rosemary.

Before you get to Building A, you pass what they call Activities G. That stands for girls' activities, and it's more like a shed than a real building. It has this one huge room that's used for a gym but gets converted to an auditorium by setting up folding chairs. There's a permanent stage at one end. I could see through the high windows that the ceiling lights were on, so I decided to go in there first.

There were five kids on the stage, two of them boys, and Miss Henderson, who was the nurse and a sort of all-around assistant to everybody, was sitting on the only chair in the room, facing the stage. She was holding onto a kind of notebook and looking from it to the kids.

"Billy, your cue is when Ginny says, 'No, no, Daddy.' "

Billy looked like he was ready to die of embarrassment; it was obvious that Miss Henderson was directing a play, and Billy was supposed to be Ginny's father.

A couple of kids giggled, and Miss Henderson said, "Now let's go through that again from Ginny's line."

"No, no, Daddy." I didn't think Ginny was convincing.

"I'm sorry, child," Billy said in a very unnatural voice, and I wondered if these were the only volunteers Miss Henderson was able to round up.

"I know Lila didn't take it." That was Ginny again. "Lila, come in and tell Daddy."

Lila came on stage, and it was Mildred. She looked at Billy and said, "I didn't take it Mr. Lawson, but if you want me to leave your employ, I will go at once."

I nearly fell over! Mildred said all that at one time and with expression!

"No, no, Lila." Ginny didn't sound any more convincing than she did the first time.

Then Mildred, as Lila, put her arms around Ginny and comforted her. Billy stuck out his arm, pointed a finger, and croaked out, "Go!"

Lila patted Ginny's head and walked off the stage with supreme dignity. I started clapping. Miss Henderson turned toward the back of the room where I was standing.

"Rebekah! Rebekah Blount, how nice to see you."

I winced when she said that name. It wasn't mine. Then I heard Mildred. "Rebekah!" She had come back on stage and was running down the steps to where she spotted me. "Oh, Rebekah." In half a second we were hugging each other. I felt like an idiot because I knew I was crying. Oh boy, the tears were gushing. I mean like you could *swim* in them. I was real proud of Mildred's self-control; she didn't break down like I did. Finally, we pulled away from each other and Mildred said, "Miss Henderson, would it be okay if—if Rebekah and me. . . ."

Miss Henderson was one of the nicer ones. "Sure, Mildred. You girls go have a real nice visit."

We had our arms draped around each other's shoulders as we walked out of Activities G, and I was sniffling because I didn't have a free hand to get my handkerchief. I felt her squeeze my shoulder and then let go.

"Better get your handkerchief."

I nodded, surprised that she'd tell me that. I mean anyone would know it was what I needed, but it wasn't like Mildred to put it in words.

I blew my nose and she said, "Gee, Rebekah, I'm so glad to see you."

"Me too," I said. "Hey, Mildred, you were great on the stage just now."

She looked really pleased, as if I had paid her some fantastic compliment. "It's such fun to do! We have rehearsals twice a week, and we'll be ready to put the play on in a couple of weeks."

I was glad she was getting involved. I mean I think that helps shy people.

"Did your—Rosemary and Tom drop you off? I mean how long can you stay?"

"I got your letter, and I—just had to come."

We stopped walking, and looking into Mildred's eyes I began to feel terrible for her again. She was wagging her head from side to side, and she looked like she was really suffering. "Oh, Rebekah, isn't it awful about poor Kathy? And there's no way we can even get to visit her."

I didn't come on account of poor Kathy. I came for poor Mildred. But she didn't seem like the poor Mildred I'd known from before. I felt very confused, as if I'd just come into a game and didn't know the rules.

I said, "Maybe she won't have to be there too long."

"But in the meantime, seeing some of us would do her good." Mildred said that with confidence, as if she knew better than the doctors.

I knew she meant seeing *me* more often would do *her* good too.

"Yeah," I agreed. "What about the others? Allie and Madelaine and the rest?"

"Madelaine will probably stay with her new family, and Allie is still trying hers out. Mary Ellen's grandmother wants her—she left this morning. So that just leaves Marie and me from our old gang."

She didn't mention her mother, like what she told her about taking her out of there. You know, you'd figure Mildred would feel envious that Mary Ellen was going to her family, while she had to keep on waiting.

There was a difference in Mildred. You couldn't put your finger on it or give it a name, but it was there. What exactly had she said or done to make me sense it? Nothing dramatic, really. How can so little make it so clear that something has changed? Or is it that things are the same but you never noticed?

"How's Doreen getting along with Baker?"

"That Doreen's got nerve."

Was that admiration in her voice? "Does she bother you? I mean, like pick on you?" I was ready to tell Doreen off.

"Oh no. But the way she looks at Baker—it's like she defies her."

"So what does Baker do?"

"Just gives her sneering looks—you wouldn't believe it. It's as if she wants to avoid an argument. Like Marie said, Baker's met her match."

Well. I shrugged. "Is she around?" I wanted to meet her.

"She's out on a weekend placement. She'll be back Monday. And Baker's off for the day, so we won't be bothered by *her*. Wanna go to the dorm?"

I didn't know where else we could be alone, unless we just took a walk and the weather wasn't too comfortable for that. It was getting pretty

117

raw. I suddenly longed for a cup of Rosemary's hot chocolate.

"Yeah, let's go to the dorm," I said.

The second I opened the door, that old-age building smell filled my nostrils. I shivered without meaning to. It almost turned my stomach. I was coming back to this? But like Rosemary said, I was doing it for someone else—not for myself. I'd tell Mildred when we got upstairs.

On the way up, memories I thought were dried up and dead came back to me. That staircase used to be like a link between anything good that happened on the outside and your room, which wasn't really your own. The staircase was also the route of escape from bad experiences to the privacy of your bed, where you'd try to imagine what it would be like gone from Meacham forever. But now everything was unreal, even strange, like it was someone else who had lived through it. And yet, of course, it wasn't someone else. It was me. I felt as if there were a clamp screwed on to my temples, and it was getting tighter and tighter.

"Phew," I let out this loud sigh when we got to the second floor, as if that would make all the pressure disappear.

"Hey, you're not used to walking up stairs, are you?" Mildred laughed, thinking that I must be tired from the climb. Maybe she thought I had gotten soft from using elevators.

"Yeah, I guess that's right," I said.

For over five years I had lived in that room, but stepping into the emptiness now was like moving in a dream. I felt all at once that I didn't belong. And I was angry for feeling that way. Hadn't I made up my mind that I was coming oack to help Mildred? Yet practically every step of the way I was fighting it. I couldn't stand it a second longer, and I cried out.

"Mildred, I've come back to stay. I'm not going to leave you ever again!"

All the blood left Mildred's face, and she stood there in front of her bed, looking horrified and staring at me in total bewilderment.

"Wh—What happened, Rebekah?" Her voice was hushed. "D—Don't they w—want you any more?"

Her misunderstanding sent a pang through my chest. No! That's not right! Of course they want me. I knew that as clearly as I knew I was alive and that this wasn't a dream. That junk I had been thinking about their forgetting me for another child was just that—junk. In my right mind I knew that.

"They *do* want me!" I said it as if I thought Tom and Rosemary could hear me and I was reassuring all of us.

"Then why. . . . ?" Mildred didn't understand.

Could I tell her that I came back because I felt sorry for her? That I thought she needed a friend to keep her from shriveling up and dying in this place like I used to be afraid I would? I started to say it then stopped myself. I didn't think Mildred was dying here. And anyway, you don't tell someone that. I had been doing that to Mildred for as long as I'd known her without thinking of its effect on her. And deciding to come back? I knew it wasn't altogether because I thought Mildred needed me. Who did I think I was kidding? The real reason I ran back to Meacham was because I couldn't face sharing Rosemary and Tom's love with someone else.

But I had to tell Mildred how wrong I'd been about her.

"Mildred," my words began spilling out in a rush, "I took two buses to get here today because I thought you needed me, but you don't. Mildred, you're okay. You're a lot stronger than I ever gave you credit for."

The color came back to her face, and she was looking at me the same intense way she did when I told her I couldn't leave last August. "Rebekah, you can't come back to stay." She disregarded the praise I'd given her and went on, "You've got a home and parents. You—You don't walk out on them."

Boy. She wasn't only strong—she was smart.

"You're right, Mildred."

I looked at her as if seeing for the first time what she was really like. My judgment of Mildred— and myself—had been way off. A million light years off. More than the distance between Meacham and Hillcrest.

"Rebekah." She reached out and touched my

arm, this time shyly. "You were really going to give up your—everything you've got now—for me?" She waited for my answer, not believing a thing like that was possible.

"Aah," I waved my hand, making little of it. "I knew you'd talk me out of it."

I laughed but she didn't. She grabbed me and gave me the hardest hug I ever had in my life.

She walked me to the high gate. I had already told her about Davy coming. I could think of him as Davy now, without resentment.

"That's going to be real nice for you, Rebekah. I mean, you're an old hand at being a Lawrence. He's coming into a family with a ready-made sister."

Leave it to Mildred to point that out to me.

"Mildred, it's a cinch to get to my place by bus. If Tom can't pick you up, they'll let you use public transportation, won't they? And you can come any time." Often—very often, I hoped.

"Gee, Rebekah, I'd love that."

"And listen, Rosemary could ask Baker or Miss Crane about sleeping over. Mildred, you know what Rosemary said? We'll probably be getting a house of our own, and we'll have gobs more room and . . . it'll be great, Mildred."

We stood there just enjoying each other, and I saw right in front of my face the totally beautiful person that Mildred Watson really is.

I knew exactly how to get back. I waited diagonally opposite the bar for my bus. The raw March wind felt refreshing. Number 32, Oakdale, the sign on the bus said, and I jumped on, feeling like a pro at riding buses.

It was four-thirty when I got to Hillcrest. Davy wasn't due until five. I ran over the crusty snow. I wanted to get home before he got there so I could greet him along with Rosemary and Tom.

Rosemary and Tom and a house and a brother of my own. Whooh! That was a lot in less than a year. A lot for a whole lifetime, I'd even say.

Maybe Kathy *would* get better. Allie might even come to love her new family. And Mildred's mother might really and truly take her next year. It could happen. You shouldn't give up hope, ever. I mean, if you do that, you're lost. And even if Mildred had to stay there until she was eighteen, I knew now that she could handle it okay—because she was a winner.

The elevator had never been so slow. Ninth floor. I ran down the hall and unlocked the door.

"Hi, sweetie. Glad you got home early. How was the movie?"

I'd tell her some other time.

"Becky, give me a hand with these books, will you? I just dug them out of the trunk in our locker. They're some of mine from when I was Davy's age."

"Oh, he'll love them. He'll be thrilled to read about the old days." I pretended to be very serious, but I was as happy inside as Christopher Columbus discovering America, finding a million dollars under my pillow, and Christmas morning all rolled up in one shiny package.

About the Author

Julia First has written two previous novels for Franklin Watts, *Look Who's Beautiful!* and *Move Over, Beethoven*.

Ms. First grew up in Boston and now makes her home in a suburb there. She lives with her husband, Melvin, who is an engineer.